Wanted Dead or Alive

A year after being saved from kidnapping, Dulcie Provost is waiting for the return of her rescuer, bounty hunter Certainty Sumner. But first Sumner has to carry out one more mission – tracking down the sadistic outlaw known as the Lakota Kid.

But unbeknown to Sumner, he himself is also the quarry of an equally ruthless bounty hunter, Luther Bastian. The father of a gang member Sumner killed while rescuing Dulcie wants vengeance and has duped Bastian into believing that Sumner has turned outlaw.

Can Sumner possibly survive being hunted down by a bounty hunter as skilled and determined as himself?

Wanted
Dead or Alive

Ralph Hayes

A Black Horse Western

ROBERT HALE

© Ralph Hayes 2019
First published in Great Britain 2019

ISBN 978-0-7198-2908-6

The Crowood Press
The Stable Block
Crowood Lane
Ramsbury
Marlborough
Wiltshire SN8 2HR

www.bhwesterns.com

Robert Hale is an imprint
of The Crowood Press

Typeset by
Derek Doyle & Associates, Shaw Heath
Printed and bound in Great Britain by
4Bind Ltd, Stevenage, SG1 2XT

ONE

Amos Latham was not a forgiving man.

It had been reported to him a few months ago that his only son Duke had been cowardly murdered in the Indian Territory by a back-shooting bounty hunter named Certainty Sumner. Apparently a rancher's daughter had run off with Duke to marry him, but her father Maynard Provost had illegally hired Sumner to find the couple, dispose of Duke if necessary, and bring the runaway girl home. Sumner had ambushed Duke and the girl in a lonely place, caught Duke off guard, and murdered him for the bounty Provost paid him.

That story had been boiling inside Amos' head like acid in a closed container for almost half a year now, and he had resolved to answer his son's killing, even though he and Duke had been estranged for years and he knew very little about his recent life. But Amos was Duke's only surviving relative, and as such he was determined to defend the family name. On that brisk spring morning in April he was addressing the problem with an ex-foreman who had worked for him before Amos'

5

retirement from his hide company. The two men sat together in the plush comfort of the well-appointed book room of Amos' sprawling Victorian home outside Missoula, Montana.

'I've asked about Sumner all over this area,' the foreman Guthrie was telling Amos. He was a brawny, tough-looking man in his fifties, about a decade younger than Amos, and had a deeply lined, weathered face. 'Nobody knows where he's operating nowadays. He's an elusive man to keep track of. The local sheriff says he ranges far and wide for the targets of his guns. Lawmen keep away from him. He's very dangerous.'

'What's this with a name of Certainty? I never heard that one before.'

'His real name is Wesley. He got the nickname because he's never failed to find and kill the man he goes after. The Wanted dodger has to say "Dead or Alive", but he's never brought a man in alive.'

Amos, sitting in an overstuffed chair near Guthrie, sat forward and stared at the floor for a long moment. 'I can't imagine that Duke had a Wanted dodger on him. He was a little wild, but he steered clear of the law.'

'Provost put the bounty on Duke's head,' Guthrie reminded him. 'Nobody knows how much it was. I understand the girl – her name is Dulcie – is back on the ranch.'

Amos let a long breath out. 'It was his daughter. When he hired that yellow-belly Sumner he probably figured he could get the girl back without gunplay. But this Sumner obviously loves killing. I have no plans to have it out with Provost.' He looked up at Guthrie grimly. He had silver hair and beard, but a rugged-looking body and a square, unlined face. 'But this man Sumner has made me hate bounty hunters. I'm going to find him, Guthrie. And I'm going to kill him.'

Guthrie, reclining on a long sofa across from Amos, made a grunting sound in his throat. 'You or I wouldn't have a chance against Sumner, Amos. Even if we tried an ambush. It would be much too dangerous.'

'I have no thought of exposing myself to that killer,' Amos told him. 'I want to find us somebody who can do it for me. Somebody that's as good as Sumner. I'll pay well for the service. But I want that sonofabitch dead. And if possible, I want him to go slow. To suffer for taking my son's life.'

Guthrie blew his cheeks out. 'Amos, I have to tell you this. I didn't put any credence in it, but I think you ought to hear it, anyway. It was told me by a drifter over in Omaha. He says he heard the story a different way.'

Amos frowned. 'What the hell do you mean?'

Guthrie took a deep breath. 'He says that when Duke was working on the Provost ranch for a short time, he got hung up on this Dulcie, but his interest wasn't returned. Then Duke was fired because he wouldn't back off trying to win the girl, and a short time later he found her out on the ranch somewhere, and took her with him by force. That's when Provost hired Sumner to find them, so Sumner was going after an abducted daughter.' He watched Amos' face closely. 'And last of all, that Duke was killed in a fair shoot-out by Sumner, after Sumner had re-taken her.'

7

A heavy silence fell into the room like a five-hundred-pound weight hitting the floor between them.

'For God's sake!' Amos growled at him.

'Like I said, it was just this drifter's story. A man I'd never seen before. It's probably bull-pucky, Amos. But I thought you ought to hear it.'

Amos' face slowly hardened. 'Now you listen to me, Guthrie. You and me got our story from honest sources. People we know. What you heard is goddam hogwash! I know my son was ruthlessly murdered by that killer-for-money. And I won't rest in my grave, by Jesus, until that piece of scum pays for what he did to my flesh and blood!'

Guthrie leaned forward, watching Amos' angry face. He waited a respectful moment, then spoke again. '*We* have to face facts, Amos. This man might be unkillable.'

Amos' dark eyes flashed at him. 'Nobody is unkillable, damn it. I didn't bring you in on this to tell me we can't have our vengeance on this man. When we locate him, we can throw a couple sticks of dynamite in where he sleeps. Or hire a gang of men to surround him and blast away together. There are ways.'

Guthrie shook his head. 'You couldn't find anybody stupid enough to gang up on him. They'd have to have clabber for brains. And the other thing just wouldn't work, Amos, it's just too iffy.'

'By God, I don't want to hear what we can't do!' Amos fairly yelled at him. 'I'm not giving up on this! I owe it to Duke. My only son, may he rest in peace. I'll go try to back-shoot him myself if I have to.'

'That would be suicide, Amos,' Guthrie told him.

'You don't owe it to Duke to throw your own life away.' He looked past Amos, to a sunny window across the room. The faint odour of musty, unused books came to him from the library on the nearby wall. 'I do have an idea, though.'

Amos' square face turned quizzical. 'Well, why didn't you say so? Spit it out.'

'The chance of it working is maybe a mite remote. But it's all I have.'

'For God's sake, say it!' Amos fumed.

'About a month ago, I ran into a fellow that used to work for us at the hide company. Name of Pritchard. He was one of your best riflemen when we went after the buffalo. He sat with me in a local saloon, and got on to the subject of this bounty hunter he met a couple years ago.'

'A bounty hunter?' Amos exclaimed. 'Why the hell do I want to hear about another goddam bounty hunter?'

'Just hear me out,' Guthrie continued patiently. 'He got to talking about this man named Luther Bastian. Seems this Bastian had pretty much the same reputation as Sumner. Only went after the toughest outlaws. And, like Sumner's targets, his people never saw the inside of a jail cell.'

'So he was good, this Bastian.'

'None better. Unless it was Sumner. They never met. Bastian dressed all in black, and rode a black stallion. Because of his look, some called him The Preacher. Outlaws feared him. And he had legitimate ties, too. He was a close friend of Captain Brett Mallory of the Texas Rangers. Seems they used to do some lawing together.'

'A lawman? Turned bounty hunter?'

'There was something about a younger brother getting murdered by thieves. And that stuck in his craw. Lawing had too many rules for him, I guess.'

'Well, he don't sound like no ordinary bounty man. Can we get in touch with this Bastian?'

'That should be no problem. The problem is, he's not doing that any more.'

'He gave it up?'

Guthrie nodded. 'According to your rifleman, a couple of years ago he hung up his guns and bought a small ranch down on the Rio Grande, and got himself married. There's also a boy. Not his. But he's settled into a quiet, domestic life now. And that's why I said the whole idea of getting him interested is doubtful.'

Amos sat there mulling all of that. Cracking his knuckles. Staring fiercely at a medallion design on the oriental carpet at their feet as if his entire future and its outcome was decipherable there.

'I like it,' he finally said, looking up at Guthrie. 'It might be our best chance.

Guthrie was mildly surprised. 'It's a long shot, Amos. You have to understand that. I get the idea Bastian ain't a man easily persuaded about anything. But there is something in our favour. He's not doing well on the ranch, and he might be in need of capital to keep it going.'

'I want to ride down there. You and me. Sweet-talk this Bastian and make him an offer that's hard to turn down.'

'If anybody could find Sumner and do the job, it's

10

Bastian. It was his business. Going after men that were hard to find and kill.'

Amos nodded. 'I like it more and more. When can you be ready to ride?'

'Just tell me when,' Guthrie told him.

Amos rose from his chair, looking physically impressive despite his age.

'My stable boy will have our mounts saddled by dawn. And you sleep here tonight. It will be a long day tomorrow.'

At that same moment, in a Tulsa saloon in the Indian Territory, and a world away from Montana, Certainty Sumner entered through swinging doors and stood surveying the place. It was late afternoon, and cowboys from nearby ranches and trail drifters had already gathered noisily, red-eyed from drink and gratingly loud in their inebriated exchanges, most with six-shooters hanging ostentatiously from low-slung holsters, riding spurs playing staccato notes to their excursions from mahogany bar to oak tables, gin splashing from held shot glasses.

The obese bartender and several patrons near the entrance turned to stare at the tall intruder, and there was a diminished noise for a moment in the room. He had an easy, athlete's stance and a young but impassive face that women found attractive. Long, dark hair showed under a black Stetson. He wore a dark blue corduroy jacket over a dark red vest with a lariat tie at his neck. A thick gunbelt hung on his right hip, heavy with a big Colt .45 Peacemaker partially hidden by the open

11

jacket. It had a bone grip and was the first thing you saw as he approached you. In addition to the Colt, he had a one-shot Derringer stuffed into his right boot, below his knee.

A piano player at the rear of the room had stopped playing when the noise decreased. Sumner's careful appraisal now complete, he strode over to the mahogany bar and leaned on it, away from the other drinkers there. The bartender laid a bar towel down and came over to him, eyeing him studiedly.

'A Planters Rye, barkeep, the unwatered stock.' Sardonically, in a well modulated voice. 'And about four of the hard-boiled eggs. I'll be at that nearest table over there.'

'We got the best double-rectified bust-head whiskey south of Kansas City,' the barman frowned. He squinted down on Sumner. 'Say, you look familiar, mister. You been in here before?'

'A long time ago,' Sumner said heavily.

The fat man snapped his fingers. 'I got it! You're that bounty man. Sumner, ain't it?'

Sumner was irritated. 'Keep it down,' he said in a level voice. 'And pay attention. Has a man been in here in the past week that calls himself Wild Bill Christian?'

The bartender hesitated. 'Oh. Wild Bill. Well, he used to come in here. But I ain't seen him here for a long time.' Picking up the bar towel to avoid Sumner's eyes.

Sumner made a sound in his throat. 'A friend of yours, is he?'

The other man scowled. 'Even if he was here, you

12

think I'd tell the likes of you?'

'He's a multiple killer,' Sumner said easily.

'So are you,' the barkeep retorted. By now a number of drinkers nearby were listening to the exchange. 'You was in prison for murder. The way I hear it, you're a back-shooting killer for money. Why should I help you?'

Sumner regarded him darkly, 'If I were the man you describe, you'd be dead now.' The barkeep swallowed hard.

'Like I said, the Planters and the eggs at that table. And they had better be over there in five minutes or you'll be explaining why.'

There was fear in the other man's face now. 'You'll get your order. I don't refuse nobody in here.'

'You're such a sweetheart,' Sumner said flatly. He went to the nearby table and sat there, removing the hat and laying it on the table. His hair was dark and thick, and his eyes always had a serious, pensive look. The bartender was right. He had gone to prison for multiple murder when he was only seventeen. Three drifters had raped and murdered the aunt he lived with, and made him watch. They had left him for dead, but he had lived. He had bought a gun, and tracked all three murderers down, and shot them down in cold blood. Without warning. He just wanted them dead, and he knew nothing about drawdowns. An unsympathetic sheriff sent him off to prison despite his youth.

'Sumner.'

He was jerked out of his reverie by a middle-aged man standing over his table.

'Yes?' Curiously.

13

'I overheard what you asked the barkeep. Christian was here.'

Sumner's face changed. 'Oh?'

'A couple days ago. I also saw him at the Trail's End, down the street. He was in town for a week or two. Bullying locals. Insulting their wives. Hoping somebody would draw on him. I know what he's done. But he's gone now. I'd guess he knows you're looking for him.'

'I appreciate the information, mister. Can I buy you a drink?'

'I'm due somewhere,' the fellow replied. 'The name's Walters. Good luck to you.'

'Thanks. Do you know which way he rode out?'

Walters furrowed his brow. 'No. But when he was in the Trail's End, he mentioned a cousin in Sloan's Corners. That's about a half-day's ride south of here.'

Sumner let a brief smile touch his lips. 'You've been a big help, Walters. If we meet again, I won't forget it.'

Walters had just exited the saloon when a man sitting not far away at another table called out to Sumner.

'Hey you! That barman called you Sumner. Was he right?'

Sumner sighed. This was what he always tried to avoid like the plague. 'Drink your ale,' he replied curtly.

The bartender arrived with the eggs. 'I'll be right back with the whiskey.' Watching Sumner's face warily.

'Skip the Planters. Make it a mug of your best beer,' Sumner told him.

The barkeep gave him a sour look and mumbled something to himself as he walked away. Sumner ignored him. In a moment he was back with the beer, and served it without comment to Sumner. As soon as he was finally gone, the same man from the nearby table called out again to Sumner.

'Hey, over there! Don't you hear good, Fancy Dan? Are you that back-shooting bounty man that killed Curly Quentin?'

Sumner shook his head. The man was sitting with two friends, and they were now laughing quietly among themselves. He glanced over at them, a boiled egg in his hand. 'I've never shot a man for money that I didn't give a fair chance to defend himself,' he said so the room could hear it. 'That's the truth of it. Now, let me eat my eggs in peace.'

'I heard you caught Quentin by surprise and sucker-shot him,' the big fellow persisted. He was a foreman from a nearby ranch, and was considered a wizard with the Colt Army revolver on his hip. He believed all bounty hunters were over-rated as gunslingers, and didn't deserve any reputation they had.

'You heard wrong,' Sumner said impatiently, eating an egg. He swigged a drink of the beer. 'I recommend you drop the subject.'

'Oh? You recommend?' the big man blustered.

The entire room had fallen quiet now. The bartender, leaning on the bar from behind it, was grinning. 'Don't take no crap from him, Hank!' Then shooting a look towards Sumner.

Sumner ignored both of them, trying to concentrate on eating. But then Hank rose from his chair, and stepped away from his table. One of his ranch hands eyed him with concern.

'Hank. Don't,' he said quietly.

But quick-tempered Hank's blood was up. 'I recommend you take your last swig of that beer, fancy boy, and light out of here. Now. Before I blow a hole through your liver.'

Sumner carefully laid an egg down and regarded the big man solemnly.

'Hank, if your brains were dynamite, you couldn't blow the top of your head off. Cool down and sit down.' Like talking to a child. In a calm, unruffled manner.

Hank's face reddened. 'You calling me dumb, you bounty scum! You just lost your chance to get out of here alive! Get up and go for iron!'

'Take him, Hank!' the bartender grinned.

But the ranch hands at Hank's table looked sober-faced.

Sumner was irritated. He took another drink of the beer and rose fluidly from the table, facing Hank. He glanced at the bartender. 'You, fat man. Bring me another mug. And make it dark ale this time.'

The bartender stared quizzically at him.

'You'll never taste that ale,' Hank breathed out harshly. Then he went for the Colt on his hip.

In the next few seconds it was hard for those present to follow what happened. While Hank's right hand was still drawing his revolver from its holster, Sumner drew the big Peacemaker in a move so lightning fast the eye could not follow the motion. Suddenly the gun was in his hand as if it had always been there, and while Hank's Colt was just clearing leather, three quick shots issued from the Peacemaker, in split-second sequence, the big gun roaring in the room like claps of overhead thunder.

Directly behind Hank a kerosene lamp exploded loudly, a hanging cigarette pail clattered to the floor, and a Wanted poster received a hole in the centre of the wanted man's face, setting the poster on fire. Gunsmoke hung thick in the air.

Hank, with his gun hanging now in mid-draw, stood open-jawed, not understanding why he wasn't dead. His left hand came up and gingerly felt his chest, to assure himself he wasn't hit. One of his ranch hands softly whistled between his teeth.

Off in a corner, a drinker whispered to a companion. 'Did you see that?' The bartender was staring unbelieving. 'Holy mother of God.'

Sumner twirled the Peacemaker twice forward, then let it fall backward once into its holster. Two more customers exchanged a wide-eyed look.

Hank swallowed hard, and re-holstered his gun. Sumner resumed his seat, picked up a boiled egg, and called out to the bartender again.

'How about that second drink, barkeep? I'm waiting.'

The bartender hesitated for just a moment, casting a look at the stunned Hank. Then he went for Sumner's ale. The room was otherwise still deadly silent. Hank shot an embarrassed look at the men he sat with, then without a word to them, or looking at Sumner again, he left the saloon.

A moment later, the room erupted in soft laughter.

It was almost a week later when Amos Latham and his man Guthrie arrived at the small ranch of Luther

Bastian. It was a spread of only a couple of hundred acres, and the two men rode through a small herd of fat Longhorns before they arrived at the ranch house.

It was a low-built, modest-looking place with a stables building at the back, a chicken coop and a pigsty. Chickens ran loose around the house, and there was a flower box on a narrow porch. As they rode up and stopped at a short hitching post, a young boy came out onto the dirt yard and stared at them. He was limping. 'Afternoon, strangers.' Sober-faced. Looking them over. 'I'm Jonah Spencer. What can we do for you?'

Amos looked him over. He was a bright-looking boy of about nine or ten, with sandy hair and freckles. His left leg looked permanently bent slightly at the knee. 'We're from Montana, boy. We came way down here to find Luther Bastian. Is this his place?'

Jonah frowned at them. He had already had experience with bad men in his young life, and he was suspicious of strangers. 'Yes, sir. This is the Bastian ranch. You here to buy cattle?'

'We're not cattle buyers, boy,' Guthrie spoke up curtly. 'Is Bastian here?'

Amos saw the frown deepen, so interposed quickly. 'We just got some private business with him, son. Would you get him for us?' He and Guthrie dismounted, and stood holding their mounts. But at that moment, Luther Bastian emerged from the doorway, looked them over from the porch, then came on down to the dirt yard.

He was tall, about Sumner's size, with broad shoulders and a long angular face. He looked around forty, and was obviously in good physical shape. Before he had

18

come outside he had strapped on something neither of them had seen before, a sawn-off Colt .44 in a custom, break-open holster that lay ominously across his belly, the gun that had been responsible for the deaths of many wanted men before Bastian had got married and begun the more sedate life of ranching.

'Can I help you boys?' he asked warily.

'They want to talk business with you,' Jonah blurted out.

Bastian came and laid his hand on Jonah's shoulder. 'What kind of business?' he asked the two men.

Amos stepped up and proffered his hand. 'I'm Amos Latham. I just closed down my hide company a while back to take life easy while I still can.'

Bastian took his hand reluctantly, and Amos noticed the iron in the grip. 'This boy here used to work for me, name of Guthrie.'

'Pleasured,' Guthrie muttered. 'I never seen a gun wore like that before.'

'It was just a personal whim,' Bastian offered. He looked back to Amos. 'Why would a hide man come to a cattle ranch to do business?'

'Well. It's a private matter,' Amos said. 'Could we sit and talk about it over a cup of coffee?'

Bastian looked them over again, and at their guns. He nodded. 'But leave the hardware on your mounts.'

The two men exchanged a look, then Amos replied. 'Hey. No problem, Luther. May I call you Luther?'

Bastian nodded again. They disarmed themselves and left their sidearms in saddle-bags. 'Jonah. Why don't you go feed the animals while these gentlemen and I

19

have a palaver?'

'Oh, damn,' Jonah complained.

'You go on now.'

A moment later the threesome entered the parlour of Bastian's house, and the visitors were impressed with its looks. There were curtains and potted plants at windows and carpets on the floor. There was a sofa and chairs, and one wall housed shelves with books. Before any of them could sit down, a young woman entered the room from a kitchen, stopping when she saw the visitors. She was auburn-haired with green eyes and a trim figure, and was about a decade younger than Bastian. Both men stared at her good looks.

'Oh. This is my wife Maggie,' Bastian told them. He told her their names.

'They're here to talk business. Can you heat them up a pot of coffee?'

'Pleased to meet you, gentlemen,' lovely Maggie told them, looking them over curiously. 'I'll just put the pot on.'

As she left the room the two newcomers exchanged a look before they seated themselves on the sofa. 'Nice-looking woman you got yourself there, Luther,' Amos offered.

Bastian pulled up a soft chair to face them. 'Met her in the Indian Territory. She worked in a clinic. Jonah is her nephew, but we treat him like a son. What can I help you with today?'

Amos laced his thick fingers together. 'We know your background, Luther. You spent much of your life doing something a bit more dangerous than ranching.'

Bastian studied Amos silently for a moment. 'You heard that way up in Montana?'

'Lawmen know your name everywhere I've been,' Guthrie said. 'Lawmen never liked me,' Bastian said.

'You took on a job for the Texas Rangers,' Amos reminded him.

'That was different. Brett Mallory and I go way back.'

Maggie brought the coffee in and set it on a tray between them, looked them over again, and returned to the kitchen. They all took a moment to take a sip of hot coffee. Finally, Amos spoke again.

'We hear you were very good at what you did.'

Bastian sipped the coffee. 'I made some money. It grub-staked me to get this place going. I was ready to make myself a new life.'

Before Amos could respond, young Jonah came in accompanied by a middle-aged, pot-bellied Latino.

'I got the chores done, Luther,' the boy announced.

'He will be telling us what to do one of these days,' the Mexican told Bastian.

Bastian smiled at them. 'You go to your room and get those arithmetic problems done, while we talk here,' he said to Jonah.

Jonah looked disappointed again. 'All right, Luther.'

When he was gone, Bastian turned back to the two visitors. 'This is my only ranch hand, Nardo,' he told them. 'He does most of the work around here.'

'*No es verdad,*' Nardo protested. He glanced at the two men. 'You come to buy our excellent cattle? We make you a good price.' He was swarthy, with a weathered but pleasant face.

21

'We're just palavering.' Bastian said.

Nardo nodded. *'Bienvenidos, muchachos,'* he grinned. 'Well. I will now go help the *esposa* with her potatoes. *Mucha gusto.'* He nodded to the visitors as he left the room.

'I'd be lost here without him,' Bastian commented. 'And he's like an older uncle to Jonah. He's like a nurse with Jonah's leg.'

'We saw him limping,' Amos said. 'Was he born with it?'

'No, no. He fell off his horse just a few months ago, and the bone healed crooked.' He sighed. 'There's a doctor in Austin that says he can re-break it and make it right again. But he's very expensive, and I can't do it right now. We're barely breaking even with the ranch.'

Amos and Guthrie exchanged a look without Bastian seeing it. Amos cleared his throat. 'Maybe I could help with that,' he said slowly.

Bastian furrowed his brow. 'You offering to hire me to go after somebody? I gave that up for good. And made Maggie very happy.'

'You could do us and your boy a favour at the same time,' Guthrie put in rather bluntly.

Bastian cast a hard look at him.

'Excuse our brashness,' Amos went on. 'But I have a score to settle and I think you might be the only one who can handle it.'

'A score?'

'Another bounty hunter murdered my boy. Just a few months ago. Shot him down in cold blood. I want his murder answered.'

'You want him killed,' Bastian suggested.

'That's it. If that sonofabitch don't go to hell, there ain't no use having one.'

'Is he wanted by the law?'

'No, the law didn't pay any attention to it.'

Bastian was shaking his head. 'Even if I was still doing this, I wouldn't go after a man unless he had a bounty on him.'

'The bounty would come from me,' Amos said.

'That's not the same. That's vengeance. Not justice. Who is this man you want killed?'

'They call him Certainty Sumner,' Guthrie answered for him.

'Sumner?' Bastian laughed in his throat. 'You want me to go find and kill Wesley Sumner?'

'Is that a problem?' Amos frowned. 'I hear you were the best.'

'Only Wyatt Earp is as good as Sumner,' Bastian said. 'And even if that didn't bother me, I've never heard a bad word about him. I'm sorry about your son, but I'd check into that story again if I were you. That doesn't sound like Sumner.'

Amos was frustrated. 'The story is true, by Jesus. I got it from a good source. Sumner ambushed Duke and shot him down in cold blood.'

'Was there a bounty on his head?' Bastian asked.

'There wasn't no bounty. There was a murder-for-hire contract put on Duke by the man he used to work for, because his daughter ran off with Duke. Sumner accepted the contract and he wantonly murdered my son.'

'And you want me to accept the same kind of contract now. With no bounty on Sumner.'

'This is different. Sumner is a murderer. My son wasn't.'

'Well,' Bastian said, taking a deep breath. 'With all due respect, Amos, I have no idea who your son was or what he was like. Even if I was still doing that for my living, I'd turn you down. I'm a rancher now. And happy to be away from that. Why don't you ask around? There are men out there who might be interested in committing suicide.'

'Suicide?' Guthrie frowned.

'There's nobody out there can beat Sumner. I've never been beat, but I wouldn't want to try it.' He rose. 'Sorry I can't help you, gentlemen.'

They both got up reluctantly, and Amos made a last plea. 'Think of your boy,' he said suggestively.

Bastian gave him an acid look. 'I think we're through here,' he responded.

TWO

It was a sunny spring day on the Provost ranch. Pasture land was erupting with the pastel hues of wildflowers, and cattle were beginning to fatten with better grazing. Dulcie Provost, the girl Sumner had rescued from Duke Pritchard and his gang last summer, was working in the stables curry-combing a few of the working quarter-horses.

It was many months since her brief time with Sumner, but she thought of him every day. In the time between her abduction rescue and her arrival back home, during which Latham was killed when he attempted to ambush them, Dulcie had very quickly fallen in love with Sumner. The trouble was, she had been only sixteen, and Sumner had not allowed himself to take her seriously. But he had promised her that he would return to her within a year, and revive their precipitous friendship.

Dulcie came out into the sunlight from the stables carrying a pail of dirty water which she emptied on to the ground. She was the prettiest girl in five counties, and every bit a woman now. She filled out her clothing

25

in a way that made men take a second look.

As she was about to return inside, a young man rode up and dismounted just a few feet away. 'Dulcie! I thought I'd find you out here!' He came over to her grinning, and gave her a big hug while she still had the pail in hand.

He started to kiss her, but she pulled back. 'Judd! I'm all messy from the stables!' Her long dark hair was shoulder length and like Maggie Bastian, her eyes were the dark green of a subtropical forest.

He was still holding her shoulders. 'I was just busting to get here, Dulcie!' He had been courting Dulcie without encouragement for several months, almost from the time she had been brought home by Sumner.

'I've got big news. Well, I hope you think it's as big as I do.' He was a stocky, sandy-haired young man just a couple of years older than Dulcie, and had a roundish, pleasant face. He took a deep breath in. 'I just got through speaking with your father. He gave me his permission. I want to marry you, Dulcie!' Like he was delivering a gift to her that should make her thrilled to receive.

Dulcie put the pail down, and frowned at him. 'Marry? You want to *marry* me, Judd?'

'Like I've never wanted anything else in my life! I've been talking it over with my folks.' He was from a neighbouring ranch. 'They like you, Dulcie. They said I couldn't make a better choice. My mom even has a couple of things to give you for the wedding. And they're all right with Maynard's church. Isn't it exciting?'

'Good Lord, Judd. You've never said anything about marriage.' Sober-faced. She went and leaned against the stables doorway.

He came over to her, the grin gone. 'You've known how I think about you for some time, sweetheart.' A small frown etched itself on to his boyish face. 'You will marry me, won't you? Dulcie?'

Dulcie sighed. 'I think you've taken a lot for granted, Judd. I like you a lot. But I'm not ready to think about marriage. I'm just not ready.'

He was frowning more heavily now. 'Now wait a damn minute here. I thought we had an understanding. I mean, why do you think I was coming over here to see you every time I got a break from droving and fencing? You're the only girl I would ever want.'

Dulcie looked away. 'I'm sorry to disappoint you, Judd. I really am. If I had had any idea.'

Anger now erupted on to his face. He picked up her discarded pail and hurled it against the side of the building. Breathing hard. Not looking at her. Dulcie jumped slightly, but did not speak.

'I don't know what's in that head of yours, girl! Do you want to look around some more, is that it? Well, just remember, you might never get a second offer! You're not the Queen of Sheba, you know!'

Dulcie gave him a solemn look. 'Why don't you go on home and cool off, Judd? I don't think I like you like this.'

He quickly mounted his dun mare and scowled down at her. 'That suits me right down to my boots! And I don't know when you'll ever see me again!' Then he spurred his mount hard and rode off, kicking up dust in the yard.

While Dulcie was still standing there feeling glum about the encounter, Maynard Provost appeared outside the house, and walked over to her.

'Judd just rode out of here like there was a hornet under his saddle. You must have said no.'

She went to him and threw her arms over his broad shoulders. 'Oh, Papa!' Her lovely eyes were moist. 'I'm only seventeen and life is so complicated!'

He grinned. He was a big man, a widower with a lined face from trail droving and silver hair. 'That's when it is complicated,' he said gently.

She released him. 'I know you like Judd, Papa. But I think you should be in love if you're going to get married.'

'And you're not,' he said.

She met his look. 'Not with Judd.'

Provost arched his brow. Then understanding showed in his square face. 'Oh. It's still Wesley Sumner, ain't it?'

Dulcie looked down. 'I know you think I'm being silly. But I can't help it. He felt something for me, Papa. I know it. And he said he'd come back. Within a year.' She crossed her arms over her breasts. 'The year isn't up.'

Provost shook his head. They went and stood against the stables wall together. 'You were only sixteen, Dulcie. I can see the attraction a man like Sumner would have for a young girl.'

'I feel just the same as I did last year,' she told him. 'It

28

doesn't go away. Sometimes I wish it would. But I have to know. If he comes back.'

Provost looked out over the prairie beyond the fences. 'Sumner isn't like us, daughter. He's a breed apart. I know that the men he goes after are deadly killers. But he's a killer himself, Dulcie. He's making his way through life with his gun.'

'I know all that.'

'He did me a favour I can never repay, in bringing you back to me alive. And if he returned here to sweep you off your feet, I wouldn't stand in his way. But I don't think that will happen, darling. He's a kind of wild thing, like the mustangs that run free west of here. He's not the marrying type. Don't wait for him too long. It could spoil your chance to make a life for yourself.'

She nodded soberly. 'I won't.'

He turned to face her. 'There's no way to put this gently. In his way of living, Dulcie, he could be dead already.'

Dulcie met his gaze with a steady one. 'He's not dead. I'd know it if he were dead.'

Provost nodded. He took her by the arm, and they walked back to the house together.

That same evening, in a crossroads cowtown in the Indian Territory called Sloan's Corners, Certainty Sumner was registering at the Two Gringos Hotel.

It was a dingy place with a wilted potted palm just inside the door, and the smell of ammonia in the reception area. Sumner had gone there on the suggestion of the friendly stranger in the saloon at Tulsa, hoping to get a lead on a very deadly wanted man called Wild Bill Christian. Christian was wanted for multiple murders in Kansas, Texas and the Territory. There were dodgers on him from all three areas because of killings in bank and stage hold-ups. Christian was known to kill without any good reason, and appeared to enjoy it. Lawmen avoided him because he was so good with the Schofield .45 he was never without.

At that moment in the hotel, a bespectacled clerk appeared from a door behind the registration desk and looked Sumner over diffidently.

'Can I rent you a room for the night, mister?'

'Yes, one night,' Sumner told him. He was dressed as he had been in Tulsa, with the dark blue jacket, but was wearing a long grey riding coat over it. He looked to a doorway to his left. 'I see you have a small dining room over there. Is the food edible?'

The clerk frowned at him and looked him over again. 'Our cook has the best beef stew in the Territory, mister. Would you sign the book, please?'

Sumner signed John Smith and looked the register over, and found it. 'I see you have a William Christian listed here. Came two nights ago. Is he still here?'

The clerk's frown deepened. 'You're not supposed to search our register, Mr Smith. We keep our clients' business confidential.'

'He's still here, isn't he?' Sumner said evenly.

The clerk hesitated, looking into Sumner's suddenly very serious eyes. 'Sometimes guests check out without telling us. So I can't say for sure.'

Sumner nodded, accepting the coded affirmative

response. 'Is there a hostelry nearby?'

A sober nod. 'Right down the street, Mr Smith.'

Sumner nodded. 'Is the dining room still open?'

'Yes, till nine.'

'I'll take my stuff up later. I might try some of that stew while there's some left.'

'I'll have your key ready, sir.'

Sumner walked into the small dining room. There was just a handful of bare, Spartan tables without cloths, and the odour of cooking food from the kitchen. An elderly woman sat at a corner table, and almost in front of Sumner there was a tough-looking man sitting alone and wearing a badge. He looked up when Sumner entered, and a look of recognition came over his bony features. Sumner was about to take a table nearby when the lawman spoke to him.

'Certainty Sumner.'

Sumner had seen the star on his chest, and sighed inwardly.

'Marshal.'

The fellow grinned. 'You obviously don't remember. I met you in Tombstone a couple years ago when I was setting with Earp. He asked you to disarm yourself and you complied. I think you looked dangerous to him.' Another grin.

'Wyatt and I got along,' Sumner said quietly. 'We had met before.'

'If you're alone, why don't you join me?

Sumner hesitated then sat down with him. 'I hear the beef stew is edible.'

The marshal was enjoying a rib-eye steak. 'Ned! Bring

this gentleman a plate of that stew you brag so much about!' A man in a soiled apron nodded and disappeared into the kitchen.

'Sorry I didn't recognize you,' Sumner told him, removing the black Stetson from rumpled long hair, and the riding coat. 'I see a lot of people in a year.'

'Since that day in Tombstone, I went to work for someone you know. Between lawing jobs. You remember Maynard Provost, I guess.'

Sumner's face changed, curiosity coming over it. 'Of course I remember.'

'I learned a lot about you while I was there. You saved his daughter from that low-life Duke Latham. Provost told me all about it.'

'It was just another job,' Sumner said, but knowing that wasn't true.

'Not according to his daughter. She couldn't quit talking about you. Dulcie, ain't it? That's some seventeen-year-old, Sumner. She thinks you're coming back there. I think she hopes you are.'

Sumner stared past the lawman to the opposite wall, as if those past days might be written on it there. In recent months he had begun thinking more and more about his promise to Dulcie, that he would ride back there within the year and try to find out how they felt about each other. As a voluptuous sixteen-year-old she had tried to seduce him in a hotel room on the way back to Nebraska, but Sumner would have none of it. She was just a kid to him. Now, he had resolved to keep his promise to her after taking a couple more bounties and giving himself a substantial bank account in Fort Griffin.

'I'll see how it goes,' Sumner answered him curtly, not liking it that this stranger knew about Dulcie.

'I wouldn't ask how you feel about going back.' A sly look.

'Thanks,' Sumner replied, looking away.

The waiter came with Sumner's order, and then came back with a dark ale for him, before the marshal spoke again.

'I know why you're here,' he finally said, forking up the last of his steak. 'He was here in this dining room last night.'

Sumner looked up at him. 'Why didn't you arrest him?'

The marshal sighed. 'He has another man with him. A boy named Pruitt, also wanted for murder. They're both fast with them sidearms. Together, they're unbeatable. I decided against suicide, as you might guess.'

Sumner grunted. 'Have you seen them anywhere else?'

'Oh, they're still in town. In saloons. They were seen in the Territorial Bank yesterday. Looking it over. The last time Christian robbed a bank he killed three people just because he didn't like the way they looked at him. I can't go up against that, Sumner. I don't even have a deputy. This is a one-horse town and I'm the only horse that can take him on.'

'I understand,' Sumner said, eating his stew.

'I hear tell he knows you're after him. But I don't think he would know you're here yet. He was heard to say he's going to blast your liver out through your back and then have it for supper.'

Sumner smiled and kept eating.

The marshal leaned forward. 'Look. You'd be doing this town a big favour if you managed to kill that sonofabitch. But to pull it off you'll have to outfox him. Don't go up against those two deadly guns in a face-down. Ambush them and back-shoot them. It's the only way. After all, they're wanted dead or alive.'

Sumner stopped eating and stared hard at the other man. 'I don't work that way, Marshal. But thanks for the advice.'

The marshal looked chagrined. 'Well. It was just a suggestion. I can tell you one thing. There's nothing Christian would like better than to lay for you in some dark alley. You might have to play by his rules to take him.'

'I never have yet,' Sumner responded.

Giving up on trying to help Sumner, the marshal got up and left without further comment. Or offer to help.

Sumner stopped at both of the town's saloons that evening but Christian wasn't at either one. And he didn't show up at the hotel that night. Sumner figured he had concluded that Sumner was in town and had found other lodgings.

It turned out he was right. The following morning, in a small boarding house down the street from the hotel, Christian was sitting in the parlour off the reception area nursing a cup of coffee and letting thoughts of Sumner run wild through his head. Thinking of ways to kill him with the least danger to himself. And with the most excruciating pain delivered to Sumner before he expired.

Christian was just under Sumner's six foot in height, but brawny, with the face of a beat-up boxer. There was an ugly scar running across his right cheek where he had also lost part of that ear. He had eschewed the more common Colt revolver for a Schofield .45, which delivered a big punch with accuracy, and it hung menacingly on his belt now. He had a long string of murders behind him that stretched back over a decade. Three of his many killings had been of lawmen, who were his favourite victims. Years ago he had travelled with a Wild West show as an expert shooter, and had taken on his nickname at that time.

As he finished his coffee, alone in the room, a second man walked in and came over to him. 'Oh. There you are. I tried your room.'

He was Rex Pruitt, and he had partnered up with Christian in Tulsa with the idea of robbing banks together throughout the Territory. He was wanted for murder and rape in Missouri and Kansas, and at an early age had purposely drowned a younger brother in an argument. He was a bit taller than Christian and slimmer, and had a wandering left eye. On his gunbelt he wore a Joslyn .44 with a firing pin that gave the gun a hair trigger. He reputedly had made the outlaw Joaquin Murietta back down in a face-down in Laramie, Wyoming.

He sat down on a chair facing Christian. 'I like the bank. No armed guards. An open safe. We can be in and out of there in ten minutes.'

Christian nodded. 'There was that little clerk, too. I thought we'd take her with us. The one with the blonde hair. We could make that entertainment last a week, where we're headed.'

'We don't need the trouble that would make,' Pruitt pointed out.

Sudden, unwarranted anger took hold of Christian's face. 'Are you telling me how to take a bank, smart boy? Are you running this show?'

Pruitt narrowed his hard eyes on him. He was still assessing whether he was right in joining up with this emotionally questionable man. 'I'm just saying. It's better if the law only has the money to think about.'

'Well, when we get in there, you do your thing and I'll do mine,' Christian said harshly, cooling down. 'Are you ready to do it tomorrow morning?'

'I'm past ready.'

'Tonight we're going to look for Sumner.'

Pruitt grunted. 'I'm still with you on that. I hate bounty hunters. I think my preference is to find him in some dark place and just back-shoot him. It's quick and easy, with no chance of anything going wrong.'

Christian stared out through a nearby window. 'I been hearing about this bastard and his blowed-up reputation for a couple years now. No, I'd like a face-down. With the two of us, he'd be dead meat. Both of us can probably beat him. We'll fill him so full of lead they'll have to get a winch to haul his carcass off the ground.'

Pruitt forced a grin. 'We'll start looking right after we eat tonight. We'll have to be careful. He'll be looking for you, too.'

'I'm always careful,' Christian said. He intended to dump Pruitt after the bank job. He had too many ideas of his own. 'Now. Let's go take a second look at that bank.'

Down the street on the other side, Certainty Sumner was just telling the hotel clerk that he wouldn't be staying the night. He was sure he would find Christian that day, and then, with a little luck, he would be riding out.

He stepped out on to the hotel porch, feeling the sun on him, and casually glanced down towards the boarding house across the street, where he intended to check later for Christian.

Christian and Pruitt were just emerging from the house. 'I'll be damned,' Sumner muttered.

Across the street, Christian spotted Sumner first. 'Well. Look at this,' he purred.

Pruitt's face sobered. 'Good God. That's him.'

Christian's ugly face settled into hard lines. 'As if by order,' he grated out. 'This is it.' He took a very deep breath in. 'When I get out on to the street, put some distance between us.'

Pruitt ran a hand across his mouth. Actually seeing Sumner was different from just talking about him. He nodded. 'I understand. I'm ready.'

Sumner stepped on to the street first. There were few other people out there, and those few disappeared immediately when they saw what was developing. Christian came down into the bright dirt street, and Pruitt followed, then went on past him for twenty feet, so they had Sumner flanked. Sumner walked towards them for a short distance, and stopped. They were now within talking distance.

37

'I see you have a friend, Christian.' In a shooting stance, the Peacemaker hanging like a cannon on his hip, his coat pushed back.

'We thought you might like more than one target, Sumner,' Christian called out to him. 'You enjoy the use of that Colt so much.' A hard grin.

'I thought it was you addicted to it,' Sumner responded. 'With that trail of blood you've left behind you.'

'What's that to you?' Christian growled now.

Sumner turned to Pruitt. 'I have no issue with you. Maybe you ought to take your leave of this. I'd guess you don't owe this man anything.'

'I'm not out here for him,' Pruitt said. 'I just dislike all bounty hunters. I thought I'd help get rid of one today.'

Sumner sighed. 'Are you carrying a bounty on you?'

'There's a couple. But you won't live to collect them.'

'Well, I'll add it all up later,' Sumner said easily. 'I'm taking you down, Christian. You've committed your last cold-blooded murder.'

Christian laughed an odd-sounding laugh. 'You shouldn't have come to Sloan's Corners, hot-shot. Take a good look at me. I'm the last thing you'll ever lay eyes on.'

In the next split second, both wanted men went for their guns. The street completely empty in all directions. Absolute silence encompassing the scene before the gunpowder storm. The Schofield and the Joslyn both now aimed at Sumner's heart, the guns exploded in hot fury in the morning quiet.

38

But a fractional second before those roaring discharges, Sumner's Colt had magically appeared in his hand and the Peacemaker's thunderous report assaulted ears and fiery lead punched Wild Bill in centre chest just as he fired, exploding his heart like a paper bag and blowing out a posterior rib. Christian's and Pruitt's shots almost blended into Sumner's, Christian's jarred shot striking Sumner under the left arm, grazing him there, and Pruitt's shot hitting Sumner in the left shoulder, in his semi-crouched position, instead of the chest where it had been aimed.

Pruitt fired off a second shot before Sumner could turn and fire, as Christian hit the dusty ground not far away. Sumner, though, had dived to his left, and hit the ground hard as Pruitt's second shot tore at his sleeve. He rolled once to his left then, and came up firing the Peacemaker again. Three shots in succession first tugged at Pruitt's vest, then struck him like a baseball bat in the belly and finally tore through his left eye like a hot poker and blew the crown of his skull away. Blood and grey matter sprayed out behind him, and then he hit the ground hard, where his right leg jerked once fitfully, and he was dead, his remaining eye staring unseeing into the sun overhead.

Sumner rose to his feet. The grazing hit under the arm was just a flesh wound, but stung badly now. The left shoulder wound was not much deeper, but would require medical help. A few townsfolk appeared in the street now, staring at the new corpses there. As they watched, Sumner twirled the Colt forward twice and then back into its resting place. He was bleeding at the

39

two wound sites, but he was alive. As he had expected to be.

He walked over and looked down at Christian. He had been dead before he hit the ground. As he walked over to Pruitt, the sound of soft applause reached his ears, and he turned and saw it was coming from the people on the side of the street.

He just stared at them for a long moment, as a frown crowded on to his rather handsome face. Then he turned without speaking and walked away, not looking again at the bloody carnage.

THREE

It had been a hard ride for Amos Latham from the Bastian ranch to Dallas, and he was in a foul mood when he got there. He had barely spoken to Guthrie all the way, and his mood had not lightened when they finally got hotel accommodation in the old section of town.

Amos and Latham were sitting in Amos' room at the end of that long day, talking about heading back north the next morning. Amos sat wearily on a big soft chair facing his bed, and Guthrie was on the edge of the bed, silently watching his old boss' face.

Amos sat forward and laced his thick hands together. 'I'm not giving up on this. When we get back, I want you to help me find somebody that would have a decent chance against Sumner. There must be another bounty hunter out there hungry for money. Or a retired lawman. We'll ask around. Maybe there's somebody out there as good as Bastian.'

Guthrie shook his head. 'We'll try, Amos. But off-hand I don't know of anybody.'

'We won't know till we do some looking around. Or what about that first idea we had? Of getting a kind of posse together. All good with guns. They all go for him as a team. Surround the bastard and blast away. Ambush him. I don't care how it's done. Hell, I'll go myself if I have to. I mean it.'

'I won't let you commit suicide, boss. And it might take a year to find more than one man to get involved in this. Most men good with guns know his reputation.'

Amos gave him a look. 'I don't care if it takes five years!' he said loudly. 'Are you with me in this, or not?'

Guthrie took a long breath in. 'You know the answer to that.' He looked past Amos to the opposite wall. 'Hmm. I just remembered something.'

Amos frowned at him. His hair was still sweaty on his forehead from the ride. 'Well? Let's have it.'

'A friend of mine that used to work on a ranch near here told me once that there's a man here that will print up anything you want. Legal or illegal. This friend got a false ID made up. The printer is a man named Masters, and I think his business is located around this area somewhere.'

Amos shook his grey head. 'You're making as much sense as a goddam fry cook running for governor. I don't want no fake ID. Why did you bring that up?'

'Just hear me out,' Guthrie went on patiently. 'This fellow Masters even makes up stuff like fake passports. He'll print up anything you want. If he trusts you.'

'I don't want a goddam passport or fake ID!' Amos retorted in frustration.

'We could get him to print up a fake Wanted dodger,'

Guthrie said quietly.

Amos' brow furrowed. 'What?'

Guthrie leaned forward conspiratorially. 'A fake Wanted poster on Certainty Sumner. Big reward. Dead or alive. Reciting some crime he's committed.'

Amos stared at the floor. Guthrie had finally gotten his attention. 'You can't just print up a fake dodger. Where's the authority?'

Guthrie thought for a moment. 'I know of a town marshal in a small town in Arizona Territory. North of Tombstone. Nobody even knows he's there. We'll put his name on the bottom of the poster, and I'll forge his signature. Then we'll get it printed up that way.'

'Do you know what his signature looks like?'

'No. But neither will Bastian when we present it to him.'

A slow grin edged on to Amos' weathered face. 'We take it to Bastian. Damn! His main objection before was that he had never heard anything bad about Sumner.'

'Exactly.'

The grin widened. 'You're a goddam genius, Guthrie! Let's do it! Where is this Masters located?'

'The clerk downstairs will know. We'll go first thing tomorrow.'

Amos rose from the chair with renewed energy. 'You just made this day a good one, boy.'

After a rather sleepless night for Amos, the two of them learned the location of the Masters Printing Company, which was just four blocks from the hotel. It was in a commercial block adjacent to other business buildings, and

43

looked as if at one time it had been an old warehouse.

When they walked inside, they were in a deep room dominated by two printing presses, a large one and a smaller one over against a wall. A middle-aged man was working on the large one, oiling a part. He looked up curiously when they entered.

'Boys. Can I help you?'

'We came to get a printing job done,' Guthrie answered for them.

Masters studied them for a moment. 'Do you have an appointment?' Guthrie shook his head. 'But my friend Owens sent us. He had some ID made up here. He says you're the best.'

'I don't know anybody by that name. What kind of job did you want done? This is my busy time of year.'

'We want a Wanted dodger made up,' Amos answered. 'We got a hand-done paper here to show you what we want.'

Masters took the paper and studied it. He looked up at Amos. 'This is under the authority of this Arizona marshal? Is that his signature?'

Amos sighed. 'The signature ain't real. The dodger won't be real. Let's just say we're playing a joke on a friend.'

Masters stared hard at him and then at Guthrie.

'Owens said you do stuff like this,' Guthrie said. 'For the right price.'

Masters shook his head. 'I think you got the wrong idea, gentlemen. I don't do nothing illegal here. Your friend told you wrong.'

Amos sighed. 'This wouldn't be illegal, Mr Masters.

44

Just like, unofficial. We told you, it's just a big joke on a friend that's always playing jokes on us. There's no intent to defraud. We'll tell him it's a fake, of course. After we give him a little scare.'

'And I guess this friend would be this Sumner in the poster?'

'Yes, that's it,' Guthrie replied too quickly.

Masters narrowed his eyes on him. 'Are you boys local?'

'No, no,' Amos told him. 'You'll never see us again after the job is done.'

There was a long silence in the big room then, as Masters stood there studying the handwritten sheet Amos had given him.

'Such a job would be expensive,' he finally said. 'Especially to work it in at this time of year.'

'I can afford whatever you'd charge,' Amos told him. 'In cash,' Guthrie added.

Masters pursed his lips. 'How many copies would you want?'

They hadn't even thought of that. Amos blew his cheeks out. 'Oh, just a few. It's only the one fellow we want to see it.'

Masters nodded, and laid the paper on the big machine. 'I'm taking a risk here. It will be a thousand dollars.'

Amos' brow shot up. But then he nodded. 'I can do that.'

'Payment in advance.'

'I can have it for you later today,' Amos promised him.

'You won't, of course, mention this to anybody,' Masters said pointedly.

'Of course not,' Amos assured him.

Masters sighed heavily. 'All right. I'll set it up. And I'll expect you back here this afternoon.'

'We'll be here,' Amos Latham said with a wide smile.

That next day, up in Kansas, Certainty Sumner rode into a little town called Sulphur Creek, still with no knowledge that down in Texas Amos Latham was plotting his demise.

Sumner had a nephew in Sulphur Creek, a boy of about twelve named Jock whom he hadn't seen in years. The boy was an orphan who lived as a ward with an elderly woman whom he called an aunt, but was not. Sumner had sent Jock money on occasion, to help in his upbringing, and had decided he would like to see the boy again while he was in the area. On this late spring day he rode through the quiet town to the marshal's office for information about Jock, and to renew old acquaintance. When he walked into the small clapboard building in mid-afternoon, Marshal Uriah Tate was busy at his weathered old desk. He looked up distractedly when Sumner entered.

'Can I help you?' Then he focused on Sumner. 'Well, I'll be damned. Wesley Sumner, ain't it?'

Sumner smiled at the recognition. 'The same. It's been a while, but you're looking good, Marshal.'

Tate came around the desk and shook his hand. Across from the desk was a poster board with civic announcements and Wanted dodgers tacked up on it.

There was a pot-belly stove under the board, and a gun rack down a hallway that led to a couple of holding cells. 'Good to see you again, Sumner. Your nephew was in a few weeks ago, asking if I had any news about you. He's a fine boy. Looks a lot like you, as a matter of fact.' He was a middle-aged man with greyish hair and a soft belly.

'I was in the area and thought I'd stop past and see him,' Sumner said.

Tate sat on the corner of his desk. 'Oh, that's too bad. 'That Sykes woman that looks after him went off to Wichita a couple days ago and took Jock with her. They won't be back for at least a week.'

Sumner sighed. 'Well. Maybe I'll get past on my way back through.'

'You're a kind of hero to him, you know.'

'I'm sorry to hear that.'

Tate regarded him curiously. 'I see. But the boy is doing well. He did have some trouble with a drifter not long ago, though.'

'Trouble?'

'Some low-life stranger in town was carrying a box of vittles out of the general store and Jock accidentally ran into him. The box went flying and groceries was laying all over the ground. I think that bastard would of shot him if a couple of townfolk hadn't got between him and Jock.' His face lengthened. 'He said he would find Jock his next time through here.'

Sumner's blue eyes narrowed down. 'I don't particularly like that.'

Tate looked away. 'Me and the boy been playing

47

checkers regular when he gets past here. I worry over things like that.'

Sumner sat down on a chair beside the desk, and Tate seated himself behind it again. 'But things are otherwise quiet,' Tate said, changing the subject. 'How have things been with you, young man? You look different. Maybe more mature.'

Tate didn't know on that previous visit that Sumner had decided to take up bounty hunting as a profession. Sumner looked over at him soberly. 'I hunt men down for the bounties on them,' he answered, watching the marshal's face.

Tate's eyes widened. 'Oh, my God! You're Certainty Sumner!'

Sumner smiled slightly. 'Guilty.'

'I've heard that name. I didn't put two and two together.' He looked Sumner over carefully again, and then his eyes went down to the Peacemaker that seemed to hang warningly on Sumner's gunbelt. 'Well. Won't Jock be interested in this.'

'I think he figured it out the last time,' Sumner admitted.

Tate nodded. 'That makes sense. So. Are you on the hunt now, Sumner?'

Sumner shook his head. 'I just finished one. In fact, I'm not sure how much longer I'm going to be doing this.'

Tate showed curiosity. 'Thinking of quitting then?'

'It's possible. There's this girl.'

Tate grinned. 'Oh, yeah. There's always a girl.'

'A rancher's daughter. Up in Nebraska She was

48

abducted by some jackass named Latham, and I went and got her. She got the crazy notion that she was falling in love with her rescuer. But that's natural. And she was only sixteen.'

'And now you want to find out if she still feels the same way?'

Sumner smiled again. 'I know it's probably all peyote smoke. But I kind of promised her I'd be back.'

'If it works out, you'd give up bounty work for her?'

Sumner sighed. 'I'm about ready, anyway, Marshal. I have a nice little nest egg in a bank in Kansas City now. And one of these days I'll lose the edge I've had, to do this successfully.'

'If what I've heard about you is true, I doubt you'd convince many folks in these parts that you'll be losing any edge. In fact, I'd think there are some really bad men out there that will celebrate with a big party if you hang up that Colt.'

'Most lawmen don't speak so kindly of me.'

Tate nodded. 'There are some bounty men that should be in jail themselves. But I've never seen or heard anything about you I didn't like. And having said that, I hope that girl still has a hankering for you. I think she'd be getting something worthwhile.'

'That means something, coming from you, Marshal.'

At that moment, a scraggly-looking man came through the door, and he was wearing a badge, too. He was rather thin, with a sallow face, and his clothing looked wrinkled and soiled. He stopped at the desk, and glanced sourly at Sumner.

'I checked out that complaint at the Lost Dogie. It

wasn't nothing.'

Tate nodded. 'This is my deputy Webster, Sumner. Webster, this here is Certainty Sumner.' Watching Webster's face for his reaction.

Webster frowned heavily. 'The bounty hunter?'

'That's right,' Sumner told him.

Webster looked outraged. He hurled a hard look at Tate. 'You're sitting and palavering with a damned bounty man? Is he under arrest?'

'Of course not,' Tate said acidly. 'Sumner is one of the good ones, Webster. He's Jock Sumner's uncle.'

Webster was studying Sumner with rheumy eyes. 'Well. I don't get it. But you're the boss, Uriah.'

'Yes, thank God,' Tate muttered. 'Go find something to do out back, Webster. There's a bed needs changing back there.'

Webster gave Sumner a last sour look and disappeared down the hall.

Tate was shaking his head. 'Don't pay him no mind. He's got horse-pucky for brains. Before I hired him, he was cleaning stables for a living. But nobody else wanted the job.'

'He's no worse than some sheriffs,' Sumner told him.

'I'll replace him the minute somebody shows up that can actually use a gun,' Tate sighed. 'Say, what will you be doing for a living if you really take that girl on?'

Sumner stared past Tate. 'First of all, Dulcie is probably married by now. Anybody that looks that good to men won't last long. And ranch girls marry early.' He paused, letting memories of Dulcie fly around in his head. 'But to answer your question. I worked for Clay

50

Allison on his ranch a few years ago. I could probably do that for her father. If he'd have me.'

'You hung out with Clay Allison? The notorious gun-fighter?'

'He taught me how to shoot,' Sumner said.

Tate shook his head. 'I've heard some stories about that man.'

'Not many are true. I liked him.'

'I can't imagine you as a rancher. Hell, I could use you right here. As my deputy. Be a chance to get rid of Webster. You could end up marshal here when I give it up. And you have Jock here.'

Sumner smiled at that. 'I can't imagine me as a lawman, either. But we can't know what the future might bring, can we? Maybe it's just as well.'

'Maybe. But you could turn this office into something to be proud of. Anyway, I hope. . . .'

The front door opened again, and it was a fellow from the local post office. He was thin, with pock-marks on his lower face. He wore a green visor.

'Weeks,' Tate greeted him. 'What you got there?'

Weeks delivered a thin sheaf of papers to Tate. 'This just come in the mail. It's a new Wanted poster on some character that could be headed for Kansas. You're supposed to post it soon as possible.'

Tate nodded. 'I'll do that, Weeks. Thanks for bringing them.'

A moment later the thin man was gone, and Tate was glancing at the dodgers. Sumner rose from the chair.

'Well. This is getting to be like the train station in Wichita. I'll be riding on out now, Marshal. Tell Jock I'll

51

see him when I get back past here. I'd like to see the boy again.'

Tate held a hand up. 'Wait a minute, Sumner.'

Sumner frowned. 'Everything all right?'

'This Wanted dodger. I recognize the drawing on it. And the name. Remember that fellow I mentioned that had a ruckus with Jock? By God, this is him.'

Sumner sat back down. 'Are you sure?'

'I remember somebody in a saloon saying his name. He's called the Lakota Kid, nobody knows his real name. Part Indian, I guess. He was already wanted for murder in Wyoming when he was here, but we didn't know that. Now he's killed a whole stage coach full of passengers, four plus the driver. There was nobody on shotgun. Two of the passengers were women.'

'Sonofabitch,' Sumner muttered.

'He's considered deadly with his gun.' He watched Sumner's face. 'And he's the bastard that threatened Jock.'

Sumner nodded. 'How much are they paying for him?'

'Five thousand dollars,' Tate replied pointedly.

'Dead or alive?'

'Dead or alive.'

Sumner nodded thoughtfully. 'May I see it?'

Tate handed a copy of the new dodger to him. When Sumner took it with his left hand, he winced slightly. There was a thick bandage under his shirt from the shoulder wound received against Christian and his cohort.

'You all right?'

'Just a product of the business I'm in. It's healing well.'

Tate shook his head while Sumner studied the poster. After a moment he looked up at Tate. 'Can you spare this?'

'Take it,' Tate told him. 'Nobody around here will be interested.'

Sumner folded it and stuffed it into a vest pocket, under the dark jacket.

'I thought you was going to give this up.'

Sumner sighed. 'I don't like threats against my nephew. Maybe I'll make this my last job. Before I stop past the Provost ranch.'

'Well. Good luck with both of those enterprises.'

Sumner rose from his chair. 'Every man needs a little sometimes,' he offered. 'You wouldn't know where this half-breed rode off to, would you?'

Tate squinted his face up, trying to remember. 'Now that you mention it, Webster said the bartender at the Prairie Schooner heard him mention he was headed to Laramie. Of course, that could mean nothing.'

'It's the only clue I have,' Sumner said.

'Well, I guess Webster is good for something after all.' A wry smile as he stuck his hand out again. Then his face went sombre. 'Listen. Take care of yourself, Sumner.'

Sumner nodded. 'I have to in my business,' he grinned. 'Nice to meet up with you again, Marshal.'

A moment later he was gone.

It was a warm spring afternoon at the Bastian ranch. Nardo Zamora and Luther Bastian were out on the

53

range rounding up strays. Maggie and Jonah were in the house, and Maggie was taking some time to give Jonah some home schooling while her flank steak was cooking in the oven.

'Who was the president during the Civil War, Jonah? We just talked about him yesterday.'

They were seated at the dining-room table. Lovely Maggie had her hair up in a bun behind her head, and was still wearing a frilly apron. A couple of days ago a doctor who had stopped past to look at Jonah's leg had told Maggie she was pregnant, but she hadn't told Bastian yet. She was waiting for the right time, because she thought it would worry him, with their finances so low.

'That would be Mr Abraham Lincoln,' Jonah told her smugly. He had been living with Maggie just a couple of years, but loved her like a mother. Actually it had been Bastian who had brought the boy to her from Texas, when he was on his way to confront a notorious outlaw.

Maggie smiled. She loved having this precocious, likeable youngster as her own and assist in his growth. But it bothered her even more than Bastian that they couldn't immediately afford surgery on his leg.

'I knew you'd get it. We'll quit for today, and do some geography tomorrow morning.' She was about to continue when Bastian walked in, sweaty and tired-looking. 'Oh, there's Luther.' She rose as Bastian came and gave her a quick hug.

'I smell something good in the oven,' he smiled at her. He gave her a small kiss as Jonah watched, grinning. Bastian pulled away and looked her over. 'You look – different, girl. I can't quite say why. But I like it.'

Maggie took a deep breath in as Jonah left the room with a history book. 'Luther. I guess it's time I told you.'

He frowned slightly, wiping at sweat on his forehead. 'Told me what?'

But as Maggie started to respond, their man Nardo stuck his head in past a screen door at the front of the house. 'They are almost here, Luther!' Then he disappeared.

'Oh. We saw two riders coming. I didn't recognize them. They'll be here any minute. What were you going to say?'

Maggie shook her head. 'We'll talk later,' she told him, and quickly went to the kitchen to check on her cooking.

Bastian shrugged, and went outside to greet the strangers. His face changed when he recognized Amos Latham and Guthrie.

'I'll be damned,' he murmured.

In a moment the two were dismounting at his hitching rail.

'Well,' Amos smiled at him. 'I bet you didn't expect to see us back here.'

Bastian didn't return the smile. 'No. I didn't. I thought we had your proposal all talked out, Amos. What brings you back here?'

Amos and Guthrie walked up to him. 'I've got big news, Luther. News that might change your mind.'

Bastian furrowed his brow. 'What kind of news?'

'Can we discuss it inside?' Amos suggested.

'Sure. Come on in. Maggie is fixing up a nice supper in there. You can stay if you'd like.'

'Oh, we'll probably be riding on. After we palaver a spell.'

Maggie was just returning from the kitchen when they entered the parlour and a sober look settled on to her pretty face when she recognized them.

'Ah. There's the missus,' Amos grinned. 'Just as pretty as we remember her.'

'Latham, isn't it?' Maggie responded without smiling.

'That's right. And here with a much more interesting situation than we had before.'

Maggie and Bastian exchanged a look. 'Why don't you take a load off, boys?' Bastian said. They seated themselves on two soft chairs. 'Can Maggie get you something?'

'No, thanks,' Amos answered. He was excited about showing Bastian the poster he had in a shirt pocket. 'But why don't you sit down too, Mrs Bastian? This would also concern you.'

'Well,' Maggie said. 'I have a few minutes.'

A moment later they were all seated, Bastian and Maggie on a long sofa facing their visitors.

'Is this still about Sumner?' Bastian asked bluntly. 'I think we've been through all that, Amos.'

'It ain't the same now as when we were here,' Guthrie spoke up in his abrupt manner. 'Show him the paper, Amos.'

Amos gave him an irritated glance. He leaned

forward on his chair, and caught Bastian's eye with an intense look. 'We know you had this impression about Sumner, despite what we told you about my son's murder.'

'Go on,' Bastian said.

But at that moment Jonah came busting into the room from a bedroom. 'I got my arithmetic done, Maggie!' He saw the two men. 'Oh.'

'That's good, Jonah,' Maggie's warm voice told him. 'Now, why don't you go out and tend that hog we were watching while we talk here?'

Jonah shrugged. 'All right, Maggie.' Then he limped away and out the front door.

'He's a brave boy,' Amos said. 'Having to deal with that.'

'It's gotten a little worse,' Bastian said heavily. 'I might have to ride to Austin to see if a bank there will make us a loan.'

Amos glanced at Guthrie. 'You shouldn't have to deal with something like this.' He paused. 'I have something you might like to see. About this Certainty Sumner. That could change everything for you.'

Bastian and Maggie both frowned, as Amos drew the fake dodger from his shirt. 'This boy ain't what you thought he was. He's a damn murderer, just like I tried to tell you.'

'Sumner? A murderer?' Bastian frowned.

'Look at this.' Amos handed the fake dodger to him, and Bastian studied it. 'This is on Sumner?'

'That's right.'

The paper read as follows:

WANTED
Wesley 'Certainty' Sumner
For Crimes in Blaney County, Arizona
Foully Murdered Family of Three
At Wells Fargo Depot
$5,000 REWARD DEAD OR ALIVE
Under Authority of Governor Richards
And Issued By
Sheriff Matt Pritchard (with signature)

Bastian looked up from the paper with a sombre expression. 'This doesn't sound like Sumner.' He handed the document to Maggie.

'I tried to tell you. He's just another bounty hunter gone bad, Luther. Like I said before. And no offence, of course.'

'None taken,' Bastian said quietly, looking off into the distance.

'I would match the amount on the dodger,' Amos said slowly. 'And you'd get that immediately. In advance.'

Maggie looked up from the paper. 'Ten thousand dollars.'

'That's right,' Guthrie put in. 'It might take you years to earn that here on your ranch.'

Amos put a hand up to silence him. 'Your boy's leg ain't going to get any better in the meantime, either,' he said quietly. 'I have complete confidence in you, boy. And you're the only hope I've got.'

Maggie looked over at Bastian. 'You said you'd never

do this again.'

He nodded. 'But I've never been in this situation before. Maggie, those banks probably aren't going to lend me as much as we need. I have to give this some serious thinking. For Jonah.'

She sighed heavily. 'Why don't we step into the kitchen for a moment? You don't mind, do you, gentlemen?'

'Not at all,' Amos replied quickly. But Guthrie was frowning now.

Bastian followed his wife into the next room, where the good cooking smells were strong. When they got there, she turned and hugged him.

'Before you make a decision on this, there's that thing I have to tell you that I mentioned before.'

He held her shoulders and looked into that lovely face he had grown such affection for. 'What is it, sweetheart?'

She took a deep breath in. 'Doctor Smyth just told me. I'm going to have a baby, Luther.'

His face showed shock. 'What?' A grin started on it. 'Is he sure?'

'He seemed to be.'

Bastian hugged her to him again, feeling a thrill ripple through him. This was what they had wanted for two years. 'My God, Maggie! We did it!'

'I thought you had to know. Because there will be even more expenses for us soon. In case that figures into your decision. I didn't want to keep that from you just to keep you here. Anyway, I'm not sure what's right. It would be wonderful to have money to fix Jonah's leg.

59

And Nardo would watch over us while you're gone. But. . . .'

'Yes?'

'Who is this Certainty Sumner?' Her face was sombre. 'And is he likely to kill you?'

He saw the new fear in those lovely green eyes. He sighed heavily. 'I won't keep it from you. He has a big reputation. He might be better than me.'

'I didn't think anybody had a bigger reputation than The Preacher,' she smiled wanly, referring to Bastian's nickname when he was carrying iron.

He took her hand in his. 'We're not doing so well money-wise, Maggie. We will, given a couple more years. Jonah's accident was just bad timing. But for one job that might take just a few weeks, we could have enough to get Jonah fixed up and coast through these lean times.'

She looked into his dark eyes. 'You're not a killer any more, Luther. I like you this way. And I prefer a bad leg on Jonah to a dead husband. I need you with me here. You could take all this away from us.'

He turned away from her, and stared out through a nearby window to the sunny day out there. 'I don't want to do this, Maggie. But I think I have to.'

She came and hugged him from behind.

'It's Jonah's whole future that's at stake,' he added quietly. 'And maybe ours.'

When he turned back to her she was crying. He kissed her lightly on her lips. 'You stay in here. I'll talk to them.'

Amos and Guthrie were waiting tensely in the other

room. They watched his face closely as he came back in. Bastian came and stood between them.

'I'll do it,' he said.

A big grin broke out onto Amos' face. 'That's my boy! I knew you couldn't turn down such an opportunity. You'll never regret it, Luther.'

Bastian wasn't smiling. 'I regret it already,' he said quietly. He sat down with them. 'You said your matching figure would be up front.'

Guthrie picked up a leather pouch he had carried in with him. 'This is it. All cash. Just like we told you.'

Bastian pulled a string and looked inside.

'Count it,' Guthrie said.

'No. It would be foolish of you to short-change me,' Bastian suggested. He hefted the bag. 'This will get that surgeon going on Jonah's leg. I appreciate it.'

'Nonsense,' Amos told him, rising. The other two followed suit. 'It's me that's getting something important here. And this money is non-refundable, no matter what happens out there.'

Bastian nodded. 'I'll depend on Arizona coming up with the rest. If it all works out.'

Guthrie gave Amos a secret glance.

'I know you'll do it,' Amos was saying. 'I got this feeling. Here's my address. So you can tell us when it's over.' He handed Bastian a slip of paper.

'You'll find out. One way or the other,' Bastian suggested.

It was less than a half-hour later when they rode out, Amos a very satisfied man. But when Maggie came into the parlour, there were tears in her eyes.

61

'I know,' he said, taking her into his arms. 'But if it helps, I've never been beat in a draw-down, Maggie. I want you to count on me being back here in a few weeks.'

She nodded tearfully. 'I will.'

'I'll be leaving tomorrow. I have no idea where Sumner might be. Maybe I'll never find him. But if I do, he'll go down. What he did in Arizona is unforgivable. He must have had that in him all the time, and it just came out. That happens to some men. And I'm the best chance there is of bringing him to justice.'

'I know.' In a whisper.

'After I'm gone I want you to take Jonah and Nardo to Austin. Get an appointment for Jonah's surgery. Don't tell him why I'm leaving. He won't want me to do this.'

'I understand.'

There was little sleep in the house that night. At an hour before dawn Maggie heard Bastian moving about, and got up to join him. He was in the kitchen, making a pot of coffee. Maggie stopped short when she saw him.

Bastian had donned the clothing he used to wear as a bounty hunter. He was all in black, except for a white shirt underneath a vest and jacket. A shortened Peacemaker .44 lay prominently across his belly, in a custom, break-open holster, and there was a Meriden five-shot pocket revolver under his left arm in a shoulder holster.

'My God. You're him again,' Maggie breathed. 'You look just like you did when I first met you at the clinic in Kiowa Junction, when you brought Jonah to me. You scared me then, and you scare me now.'

'It's just me, Maggie,' he told her. 'With different clothes.'

'And bristling with guns,' she added.

He was drinking some of the coffee. 'Don't think about the guns. Just concentrate on how much we'll enjoy seeing Jonah walk without limping. I should be back before the surgery.'

She came and hugged him. 'Oh God, Luther.'

He knew there wasn't much left to say. A few minutes later, before anyone else was up, he climbed on board his black stallion with the star on its muzzle, and rode off into the gathering dawn.

Later that day, in mid-afternoon, the Lakota Kid waited behind some high rocks on a remote section of a stage-coach trail not far from Boulder, Colorado. He liked to have a partner in such an operation, but a fellow he had been drinking with a couple days ago, and whom he expected to be with him now, had made the mistake of arguing with the Kid on some trivial matter and the Kid had blown the lobe off his right ear.

The Kid pulled an old railroad watch from a vest pocket and saw that the time was 3:10. The stage was due past here by 3:30, he figured, and he was getting impatient for its arrival.

This was not the Kid's favourite kind of job. A lot of things could go wrong in a stage hold-up. Sometimes you even had trouble from the passengers when men wanted to look like heroes to their women. Some coaches had a man riding shotgun, and some didn't. If they did, you shot the shotgun rider first. He knew a gunman who had had his head blown clean off his shoulders by a coach shotgun. This one was supposed not to have one.

He looked at the watch again. It was 3.13. Time seemed to stand still when you were waiting for something to happen. He remembered his recent stop in Sulphur Creek, Kansas, and how he had planned to rob the general store there, but had been frustrated from that objective when some stupid kid had knocked some groceries out of his hands, which had caused a crowd to gather, and spoiled the whole thing. He would get back there soon, and find the kid. Maybe give him a beating so bad he'd have trouble walking, let alone running into people. And he would make a second try at that rich store.

There was the sound of thundering hoofs coming now at a distance.

The Kid nodded. 'Right on time,' he said aloud.

He pulled a polka-dotted bandanna up over his lower face, and waited for the coach to come into view. Thoughts flying through his head. In Boulder, he had heard something that had motivated him to move on. Some drifter who had just come up from Kansas said he had heard that a man named Sumner had been asking about the Kid in a saloon in Wichita. If it was Certainty Sumner, that was not good news. The Kid had heard of that bounty hunter, and his reputation. Nobody wanted to hear that Sumner was asking about them. It was considered very bad luck.

The stagecoach was within a hundred yards now, and

coming into sight.

Suddenly the Kid rode out on to the trail, firing the Dardick 1500 .38 he always carried with him.

The coach dusted to a stop not far from him and there was no shotgun man. 'Hold it up right there!' the Kid shouted.

The four horses were snorting and guffering, very excited. The driver, a middle-aged fellow with a big nose, held his hands up.

'Don't shoot! You can have what we got!'

The Kid rode on up to him. A couple of heads had stuck out of the window of the coach.

'You got anything in that box under the seat?' the Kid asked in a quiet, pleasant voice.

'No, sir. We ain't hauled a payroll in months. You can check if you want.'

The Kid grunted, studying the man's face. 'No. I don't think you got the guts to lie to me. Listen, what's your name?'

The driver squinted his face up. 'Name? Why, it's Ross.'

'Do you believe in the afterlife, Ross?'

The heads had pulled back inside the coach now, and a middle-aged man had climbed out to look at the Lakota Kid. The Kid ignored him.

The driver licked paper-dry lips. 'Uh. Yes, sir.' Warily.

'Do you think you're going to heaven or hell?'

Now the driver could barely speak. 'I don't really know.'

'The Lakota have an expression,' the Kid went on. 'Maybe you've heard it. They say, "This is a good day to die." Do you feel that way today, Ross?'

'Now, wait,' the driver said thickly. 'I told you. You can have what you want. Just don't kill anybody.'

The man who had stepped out of the coach had narrowed his eyes down. 'Mister. I've spoken with those inside. We have some cash and jewellery. You can have it. Just don't shoot anybody.'

'Shut up,' the Kid said without looking at him. 'Now, Ross. Why don't we find out where you're going? I mean, you know, afterwards.'

'Please,' the man on the ground intervened. 'Just take our valuables and be on your way.'

The Kid ignored him. Waiting for a response from the driver. 'Or if you'd prefer, you could put it off to a day you like better.'

The driver swallowed hard, nodding. 'Yes.' Croaked out.

'Get your gun out,' the Kid ordered him. The driver hadn't disarmed.

He saw the Dardick still trained on his chest. 'My gun?'

'You know how to use it, don't you?' A slow nod.

'Yes, sir.'

'Well, then. Take your revolver out and shoot that man standing there. And I won't kill you.'

The rancher on the ground stared hard at the Kid. Inside the coach, a woman could be heard gasping. 'What the hell,' the rancher mumbled.

The driver looked from the Kid to the ranch man and back to the Kid. 'Why, I couldn't shoot Mr Philips. I known him for years.'

'I didn't ask how long you've known him.' He looked at the railroad watch again. 'When this second hand comes around to straight up again, either I shoot you or you shoot him. You have less than thirty seconds.'

'You sonofabitch,' the rancher growled.

The driver looked panicked. He pulled an old revolver on his hip and looked at it. He squinted his face up and turned the muzzle towards the rancher.

'For God's sake, Ross!' the other man said loudly.

The rancher's wife stuck her head out of a window and screamed. 'Don't! For God's sake, don't!'

Ross dropped the gun to his side. 'I can't.' In a whisper. 'I can't do it.'

The Kid laughed quietly. 'I knew it, deadhead. I was just playing with you. It was a joke. Get it?'

Ross eyed him warily, and the rancher breathed a sigh of relief.

'Don't you laugh at jokes?' the Kid was now saying soberly.

'Sure,' Ross answered almost inaudibly.

''Then why don't I hear you laughing?'

Ross caught his eye nervously. Then he tried a small laugh, but it came out as a croaking sound.

The Kid shook his head. 'Pitiful.' He was still mounted. He threw a cloth bag to the rancher. 'Pass that around in there. I'll know if you hold out on me.'

There were just the rancher's wife inside and a young man who worked for Philips. Neither the ranch hand nor Philips were armed. They collected cash and a couple of rings and handed the bag back out. Philips added more cash and a lariat clasp. The Kid examined

67

the contents, and then moved his mount up so he could look inside the coach.

'You mean this is it?'

'That's all we have,' Philips told him.

The Kid looked inside again. 'Is your woman good in bed?'

Philips' face turned red. 'I reckon that's my business.'

'If you let me take her, I won't shoot you.'

Philips shook his head. 'Then shoot me.'

The Kid laughed again. 'You folks just don't have a sense of humour around here. Well. I'm in a good mood today. I won't take your little wife. She's probably all used up, anyway.' He turned back to the driver Ross. 'But you disappointed me, Ross. And I don't like disappointment.' He raised the Dardick again and fired, and the explosion blasted a hole below Ross's left eye and made everybody's ears ring for a moment. Ross fell sidewise off the coach.

The Kid stuffed the loot bag into a saddlebag, grinned harshly at Philips, and then rode off without another word.

FOUR

It was June, and the weather was warming up. Certainty Sumner had ridden north in the hope of finding the Lakota Kid in Wyoming or Montana, and had reached a small town in western Colorado south of Denver, taking a hotel room there for the night.

Sumner had already stopped at the local marshal's office to inquire about the Kid, but without result. Now he was settled into his room, before going downstairs to a small dining room for a light supper. He was sweaty and tired, and intended to pay a dollar for a bath after he had eaten.

The shoulder dressing under his shirt had been replaced by a much smaller one, and he was feeling no pain from either wound received at the hands of Wild Bill Christian and his recruited cohort. It was about an hour before meals would be served downstairs, so he had removed his jacket and vest, but still wore the Peacemaker. The one-shot Derringer he usually carried nowadays in his right boot lay on a night stand beside the bed.

Sumner had tried to buy a Kansas City newspaper at a local store, but didn't find one there. Sumner was well read; he had taught himself to read in prison, and had read Mark Twain and Herman Melville, and had even read sonnets by Shakespeare. He read the newspapers regularly, and knew about a potential uprising by dispossessed farmers in Mexico, and that the streets of the nation's capital were getting electric lighting. Reformers and prohibitionists were starting to migrate into the West, and he understood that that would cause trouble. One day soon real law would come to the West, and men like him would be out of business. He often wondered whether the world would be a better place then.

He sat there propped on his bed, letting such thoughts run through his head. A lock of dark hair had fallen on to his forehead, giving him a rakish look. Under his grey shirt unseen were various scars of battle that most people never saw. But at a year over thirty, he had experienced more than some men do in a lifetime.

Thoughts of beautiful Dulcie Provost came tumbling at him, and he realized he was developing a deep interest in seeing her again. Through their adventure together after her abduction she had told him frankly that she was falling in love with him. But you don't get emotionally entangled with a girl of such tender years. Now that almost a year had passed, though, she would be more mature. Have better judgment. There would have been time for any immature infatuation to have evaporated and been replaced by calm, cool consideration. As Sumner had suggested to Uriah Tate, she very likely would have been courted by enamoured young men by now, and with her better judgment, might have accepted a proposal of marriage. But Sumner had made a promise to her, to return to her to see how they both felt about each other. And he had decided definitely now that he would do that after his pursuit of the Kid. Actually, the closer it came to the time he might see her again, the more anxious he became about it. Hoping that very special girl was still available.

As those thoughts flitted through his head a light knocking came at the room door. Sumner frowned and his hand went automatically to the Colt. He rose from the bed and went to the door.

'Who is it?' he called out.

'It's Marshal Yancy,' came the response.

It was the man Sumner had sat and talked with earlier about the Lakota Kid. Sumner opened the door. 'Marshal. I thought we were done for the night. Come on in.'

The marshal stepped inside, and removed a crumpled hat. 'I know. But the Denver paper just arrived, and I saw something you'll be interested in.'

Sumner nodded. 'Sit down, Marshal.'

The heavy-set lawman sat on a chair facing the bed. He had grey-streaked hair and heavy bags under his eyes. Sumner sat on the edge of the bed facing him.

'What do you have?' Sumner wondered.

'The Lakota Kid. This just happened a few days ago. He robbed a stage up near Boulder.'

'I'll be damned,' Sumner muttered. It was his best lead yet.

'It happened just a short ride out of Boulder, in an

71

area where he had cover from high rocks.'

'Was there anybody with him?'

The marshal shook his head. 'No. He does a lot of this stuff alone. I don't think anybody wants to ride with him.'

'Any details about it?'

'He killed the driver. Left the passengers alone this time. It depends on his mood at the time. He's kind of a crazy bastard. The passengers that reported it said he had a lot of fun playing a game with the driver.'

'A game?'

'Made the driver think he was going to spare him. Then he shot him anyway. Like he enjoyed that more than just killing him right off.'

'His previous record makes him seem like he's got something twisted in his head,' Sumner offered.

'He also insulted the woman present. And played a sadistic joke on her husband, too. Just to see the fear in his face. I wish we could hang that sonofabitch twice.'

'You won't be hanging him,' Sumner said quietly.

The marshal studied Sumner's handsome face. 'You got a lot of confidence for one so young.'

Sumner shrugged. 'I know he could kill me. Things happen. But if he does, he'll go down too. I've never failed to kill a man I went after.'

The marshal nodded. 'That's why some lawmen think you're a back-shooting killer for money.'

'Is that what you think, Marshal?'

The other man shook his head. 'No. I've heard stories about you. And I tend to believe them.'

Sumner let a smile cross his face. 'Pleased to hear that.'

'Listen, Sumner. This boy thinks he's the best with his gun. But he won't give you an honest draw-down if he can back-shoot you. In fact he'd probably brag more about that than if he'd out-drawn you.'

'I know his type.'

'God knows how many more people he'll kill before you find him. Or the law does.'

'It will be me,' Sumner said easily. 'I work harder at it than the law does. No offence, Marshal.'

The marshal grinned. 'I know that. The law up there thinks he may have headed north. Toward Fort Collins. You might try there next.'

'I think I will.'

The lawman rose from the chair. 'Be careful with this boy, Sumner. I kind of like you.'

Sumner rose, too. Smiling. 'That makes you one of a very select group, Marshal. A very select group.'

It was a muggy, overcast day at the Provost ranch. Provost's daughter Dulcie was upstairs in the sprawling ranch house, in her bedroom changing from her outside work clothes to a dress for dinner. She was in her underwear, looking much as she had that day in the Territory when Sumner rescued her and saw her for the first time. When he saw the exposed curves and the cleavage in the flimsy clothing, his first words had been, 'You're only sixteen?'

That had pleased her, when she thought about it later. Now, in her bedroom, she ran her hands over her breasts and inspected herself in a nearby full-length mirror. She looked about the same as she had on that memorable occasion, she thought, but with the baby look gone from her face. Her face was more mature-looking now, with more character, and it was even more beautiful.

'Where are you, Wesley?' she said aloud, standing there before the mirror.

She had fallen in love with him almost at first sight. Even though she learned very quickly that he killed men for money, there was nothing about him she didn't like. She had even tried to seduce him, in a hotel room on the way home. She practically invited him to her bed. It was very unlike her, she had had just one sexual experience in her young life. But she was in love. Sumner had rejected the invitation abruptly and with some irritation. He considered her little more than a child, despite the way she looked physically.

Now it would be different. He would see her maturity, and he would be in love with her, she was sure. If he really returned to her as he promised.

If he wasn't dead. She quickly put that awful thought out of her mind.

She was dressed for dinner a couple of moments later, and after combing out her auburn hair to shoulder length, she left her bedroom and went downstairs.

Their housekeeper had set the dining table, but indicated it would be a few minutes until the meal was served. Dulcie found her father in his library with another man.

'Oh. I didn't mean to interrupt,' she apologized.

Maynard Provost looked up from a table where he had been signing a paper. He and the visitor were seated on opposite sides of the low table. The other fellow was middle-aged, but there was youth in his face. When he looked up and saw Dulcie, his face changed and he just stared for a moment.

'Come on in, daughter,' Provost smiled at her. 'We're finished up here. Mr Walters has just contracted to buy some cattle from us. Walters, this is my girl Dulcie.'

Walters rose and made a small bow. Still staring. 'It's a great pleasure to meet you, Dulcie,' he finally told her. 'I'd never seen you before. And I must say, I'm very impressed. You must be the prettiest girl in five states.'

Dulcie was embarrassed. 'Thanks, Mr Walters. I hope you got yourself a good deal with Papa. He's a tough bargainer.'

Walters laughed. 'I found that out.'

'I'll be letting Dulcie do some of the selling one day soon now. She knows the value of our stock as well as I do. She rides the range with the boys.'

'That must be nice for the boys,' Walters commented a bit too personally.

Provost looked at Dulcie, but she wasn't blushing. 'We all get along well,' she said with a small smile. Actually, besides the suitor Judd Owens, a couple of the ranch hands had taken the risk of flirting with her when Provost wouldn't see it. But Dulcie was as cool to those advances as she had been with Owens. Even though they were a bit older than she was, they all seemed like boys to her, when compared to Wesley Sumner.

'How old are you, Dulcie?' Walters was saying then.

'I'm seventeen,' Dulcie told him, beginning to resent all the personal questions. 'Why do you ask?' Curtly.

He was not embarrassed. 'Why, it's just that you look so ... grown up, that's all. Maynard never told me he had such a grown-up daughter. I'd have been by here a lot more often!' A hearty laugh.

Dulcie frowned slightly. 'I'm afraid you'd have been disappointed, Mr Walters,' she said pleasantly.

His face sobered slowly, as Provost rose to intervene. 'She's a little young for courting,' he said, with a bit of discomfort.

'Oh, really?' Walters said, arching his thick brows. 'She seems just right to me.' Giving Dulcie a narrow grin.

Provost changed the subject. 'Well, I'll get them cattle fattened up for you, Walters. They'll be ready to move soon, and you can drive them on down to the market in Tulsa.'

'Yeah, I'm heading back there right now, as a matter of fact.'

Dulcie remembered those ugly days in the Territory last year, and those thoughts burned inside her like acid.

'Have either of you been that far south?' Walters said.

Provost sighed. 'Dulcie was down that way briefly last year.' He shot a glance at her. 'She didn't like it much.'

Walters frowned now, looking past them. 'Wait a minute! I just recalled that article in the Kansas City paper! Wasn't you taken down there by some low-lifes and had to be rescued by a gunslinger?' To Dulcie.

'She was abducted for a while, and I sent someone down to bring her back,' Provost interjected. 'Now, Walters. . . .'

Walters snapped his fingers. 'Of course! You sent one

76

of them bounty hunters after her! What was his name?'

Provost sighed heavily. He didn't really want to offend Walters, after just signing a big contract with him. 'His name was Sumner,' he replied curtly.

'Wesley Sumner,' Dulcie added proudly. 'I hope our cattle make you a lot of money, Mr Walters.'

'Wesley Sumner,' Walters said thoughtfully. Then his face brightened. 'Oh, yes! Good Jesus! I just heard that name from a lawman in Wichita! ls that the boy they call Certainty Sumner? Because he kills every man he goes after?'

'It is,' Dulcie said soberly, frowning. 'What did you hear, Mr Walters?'

Walters turned to Provost. 'I hope this boy ain't a friend of yours.'

Now Provost was frowning, too. 'We consider him such. Why?'

Walters was shaking his head. 'This might all be just third-hand rumour, of course. But the word is that the Preacher is out looking for Sumner.'

'The Preacher?' Provost wondered.

'Oh, you don't know. I think his real name is Bastian. The most feared bounty hunter in recent years. But he quit it to go ranching. Now he's come out of retirement, so to speak, to go after your man Sumner.'

'What?' Dulcie gasped out.

Walters liked her reaction. 'Oh, yes. That's the story. He's going after Sumner for the bounty on his head.'

'Bounty?' Provost frowned. 'Why would Sumner have a bounty on him? He's one of the most upright men I've ever dealt with.'

77

Dulcie was breathing shallowly. 'I don't believe it.'

'Well, this marshal could have been wrong. But if the Preacher really is going after Sumner, he's a dead man.' Casually. Watching Dulcie's face.

Suddenly Dulcie was very angry. 'Damn you! Nobody can take Wesley down! Nobody!' Then, after a moment, 'Excuse me, Papa.' And she ran from the room.

Provost was upset too, but decided to remain civil. 'You'll have to pardon my daughter, Walters. We both like Sumner, you see. And we find it hard to believe anything bad about him.'

'Sorry I mentioned it,' Walters lied.

A few minutes later he was gone, and Provost went upstairs and found Dulcie sitting in a chair by a window, staring outside. When she heard him enter, she turned to him.

'That awful man!'

He nodded. 'Sorry about all that. Dulcie, that story he heard doesn't make any sense. How would Sumner have a dodger on him? He doesn't have a mean bone in his body. I could tell it the first time I met him. And I've never heard of a bounty man going after one of his own kind. That lawman must have got his facts all wrong.'

'Or there is no lawman,' Dulcie offered. 'I don't think Walters liked the way I responded to him. He might just have decided to give me trouble. I didn't like him.'

'I didn't either. But we can't turn down his business,' Provost told her quietly. 'Listen, I'll go into Ogallala and see if I can hear anything about this. It will be all right, I know it.'

'I hope so, Papa. I worry about Wesley all the time, anyway. Some days I think I'll never see him again.'

'If he said he'll come back here I wouldn't bet against him,' Provost said to her. 'Now, put this out of your pretty head till I find out something.'

She sighed. 'That's easier said than done, Papa.'

FIVE

Certainty Sumner had stopped briefly in a small backwater town in southern Colorado to get his mount's off-fore shoe checked out. The stallion had been slightly lame through the late morning. He found a farrier at the far end of town who told him it was probably just a pebble that had worked its way under the horse's shoe, and he could get it cleaned out within the hour. So Sumner walked back to a small restaurant on the main street to get himself a quick lunch before riding on.

It was a modest little place, but looked clean, and the few patrons sitting at tables looked like respectable citizens. Sumner started to take a table near the door, but then saw the middle-aged man at a table at the rear of the room.

It was Clay Allison.

Clay Allison the notorious gunfighter. Clay Allison the man who had had stories written about him in eastern magazines. Clay Allison the fellow who had climbed into a newly dug grave with an adversary one time when they were both drunk, with both men unloading their guns into each other. That Clay Allison.

Also, the Clay Allison who had hired Sumner to work on his ranch soon after Sumner's release from prison, and who had carefully taught Sumner how to shoot a sidearm so it meant something when you fired it.

Sumner turned away from the table he had chosen and just stared for a moment. 'My God,' he muttered.

By the time he got halfway to Allison's table, Allison looked up and recognized him. He frowned hard, placed his fork down, and awaited Sumner's arrival with a shocked look on his square face.

'Well, I'll be damned,' he said softly when Sumner stood beside him. 'Is it really you, kid? I thought I'd never see you again.'

Sumner was smiling as he rarely smiled. Allison was not only his mentor, but a good friend. 'What a pleasure,' he said. 'I think about you often, Clay. That all seems like a hundred years ago now. In a different world.'

They shook hands. 'Mind if I join you?'

'Set your freight down, boy.' A big grin. He had some silver in his hair and his face was getting a little jowly, but he gave the appearance of being as hard as sacked salt. 'Have some grub with me.'

Sumner sat across from him, still studying Allison's face. 'You don't look a day older,' he told him.

Allison nodded. 'You do. And you earned yourself a title.'

'Oh, that. It's bull-pucky, as you know.'

'I'm not sure I know,' Allison smiled at him.

'I've laid in bed many a night and thought of those

81

pleasant days at your ranch,' Sumner admitted. A waiter came and he ordered a plate of stew. Then: 'What brings you clear up here, Clay? I thought you'd be working that herd of yours hard about now.'

'Oh, there's a stockyard in Denver wants to buy all I can bring them,' Allison responded. 'I just made a big deal with them and I might drive the herd up here myself. You want your old job back?'

Sumner smiled at that. 'I think I had enough of cow-punching to last me quite a while.' He looked down. 'I'm probably a mite better at what I'm doing now.'

The waiter brought the stew and they ate in silence for a couple of minutes. Then Allison spoke again.

'I knew you'd be one of the best. You were a natural. When you took Curly Quentin down, with me setting right beside you, I knew I had created something the world would have to deal with. I heard you found them two marshals that killed your friend.'

Sumner nodded. 'I found them.'

'But you didn't go back to that girl. The one that was his sister.'

'I went back to Jane. But she had already got herself married.'

Allison stopped eating for a moment. 'That's when you decided you'd try this.'

'I had no other future ahead of me.' He paused. 'I have a similar situation developing now.'

'A girl?'

Sumner nodded. 'After I find the Lakota Kid, I might go find out if there's a future for me that doesn't involve the use of this Peacemaker.'

'So you're after the Kid.'

'He's supposed to be in this area. Have you heard anything?'

Allison shook his head. 'But I hear he's dangerous.'

'They all are, aren't they?' Sumner said quietly.

Allison was finished eating. He took a deep breath in. 'Wesley, I heard something that might not have come to your ears yet.'

Sumner looked up at him.

'This was before I left Texas. And it's probably just a rumour.' He wiped at his mouth with a napkin. 'Have you ever heard of the Preacher?'

Sumner frowned. 'He was a bounty hunter, wasn't he?'

Allison nodded. 'He's been running a ranch down on the border. But the rumour is that he's strapped on his guns again. And he's coming after you.'

Sumner didn't stop eating. 'And why would that be?'

'The rumour has it that there's a reward out on you. And it's apparently too big for him to turn down.'

'Why the hell would I have a dodger on me?'

Allison shrugged. 'It sounded crazy to me. Maybe some lawman's got you mixed up with somebody else. But that's what I heard. And even if it's all peyote smoke, I thought you ought to know.'

Sumner was finished. He placed his fork down thoughtfully. 'Isn't his real name Bastian?'

'Yes, and he's a lot like you. I don't think he's ever actually arrested a man. When he went after them, they were as good as dead.' He watched Sumner's face. 'He's good, Wesley. Maybe as good as you. I wouldn't want him coming after me.'

Sumner stared past Allison, absorbing all of that. 'Whatever the mistake is, it could be explained to him.'

'I don't know. He had a reputation. When he found the man he was after, he didn't listen to explanations. There was no arguing with him. No persuasion would be listened to. He was the angel of death.'

Sumner sighed lightly. 'I think I'd like him.' A small smile.

'You probably would. Under different circumstances. Listen, I'm a little sorry I mentioned it. In case it's all nonsense. But it's the kind of thing you ought to know.'

'You did right,' Sumner said, taking a drink of a beer he had ordered. 'I'll keep my ears open.' He caught Allison's eye. 'And don't give this a second thought. I can take care of myself, Clay.'

'I've heard that,' Allison grinned at him. Then his face sobered. 'You know, this could be coming from somebody with a grudge against you.'

'Telling Bastian lies?'

'Exactly. Have you made any enemies lately? Because of some job you took on?'

'I can't think of anything recent. Almost a year ago I had it out with a boy named Latham. And he was supposed to have a father alive somewhere. A low-life family. Who knows what could have developed? But I doubt he even knows his son is dead.'

'Well, at least you won't have to watch your back,' Allison mused. 'Bastian always confronts his people head-on. Just like you.'

'Let's presume it's all horse-pucky, Clay. I have other

things on my mind at the present.'

Allison smiled at him. 'You sure you won't take that job I offered? You might have a better chance of getting back to that girl, if you did.'

Sumner returned the smile. It was nice sitting with Allison again. 'It's mighty tempting, old friend. But I think I'll stick to something I know a little bit about.'

A half hour later they parted company. Nothing more was said about bounties or Luther Bastian or the Lakota Kid.

Neither man felt they were fit topics for parting conversation.

The next morning in Dallas, Texas, not far from where Amos Latham had obtained his fraudulent wanted dodger on Certainty Sumner, Luther Bastian appeared in the office of Captain Brett Mallory of the Texas Rangers.

Bastian was headed north, because he had heard in a saloon that Sumner was last heard of in Kansas. But Dallas was not that much out of the way, and he thought his old friend Mallory might have some information on Sumner.

Bastian and Mallory went back a long way. In his early days, Bastian had worn a badge under Mallory in a small Texas town, before Bastian decided he wanted to make his own rules in bringing killers to justice, and Mallory had joined the Texas Rangers as a rookie.

Just before Bastian put his gun away and took Maggie Spencer and Jonah to his newly purchased ranch on the Rio Grande, to marry Maggie and raise cattle for a living, Mallory had persuaded Bastian to go after a gang of men who had savagely murdered a Texas Ranger in north Texas. Bastian had found and killed every one of them, and avenged the Ranger's death. In the process, he had taken Jonah to his estranged aunt Maggie, and fallen in love with her almost immediately.

On this early summer morning, Bastian found Mallory busy at his desk, behind a pile of court papers. When Bastian walked in, Mallory got a big grin on his meaty face. He was getting some grey in his hair, but still looked very physical.

'Good God, Luther! What brings you back here? I thought you were getting your cattle beefed up for a trail drive!' He came around his desk and shook Bastian's hand vigorously, then looked him over. 'What is this? The Preacher outfit? I thought you'd worn that for the last time.'

Luther was smiling. 'I'd have felt odd. Going back to this in dungarees.'

'Going back?'

Bastian nodded. He looked tall, dark and dangerous. The same look wanted men had seen as their last view of the world. The modified Peacemaker stood out boldly on his belly under his open black jacket.

'That's why I stopped past. I've taken on one last job, Brett. Can we set a minute?'

'You can have all morning if you want it. I want to get away from all this court stuff. It makes my head spin.'

They went and sat across the big oak desk from each other. In the corners behind the desk were the American flag in one corner, and the Lone Star of Texas flag in the other. Mallory pulled a drawer of the desk partway out and hoisted a foot on to it.

'Now. What's this about taking on another hunt? You got a dodger on this fellow?'

Bastian nodded, and reached into a pocket. He unfolded the fake poster Amos Latham had given him and handed it over to Mallory. Mallory began reading it casually, then his face changed.

'What the hell. This is on Certainty Sumner?'

Bastian sighed. 'I was surprised, too. But the dodger looks legitimate. It's from Arizona.'

Mallory frowned. 'This is a bit surprising, frankly. I've never met Sumner, but I've talked to a couple of lawmen about him. They say he follows all the rules. Just like you did.' He paused, and looked up at Bastian. 'He's good, Luther. Maybe as good as you.'

'I know all that,' Bastian said heavily. 'And I wouldn't even consider this, except that a man named Latham is doubling the reward, and I need the money, Brett. For an emergency.'

'Is Maggie all right?'

'Yes. It's Jonah. He has a bad leg from a fall. I have to get him surgery, and the sooner the better. And I can't afford it.'

'Oh hell, Luther. That's bad luck. Listen. I think I could lend you a thousand. To get things going.'

Bastian liked that. 'No, thanks, old friend. I got an advance from Latham.'

Mallory studied the paper again, then opened another drawer and looked through some wanted posters there. 'I don't have a copy of it here. But that might be because it's out of state.'

'I wired the marshal in Arizona,' Bastian said. 'I never got a reply. I'm proceeding as if it's real, and Sumner has gone bad. I don't know the man, so I have to go on the evidence I have. I know of a couple other bounty men that finally went outlaw. It happens. And if he did what it says there, it should be answered.'

Mallory nodded. 'It looks like the real thing to me. I've proceeded on ones that don't look this good. I see it says, dead or alive.'

'I wouldn't go, otherwise,' Bastian said.

'I know.' Shoving the drawer back. 'I know.'

'Do you know anything about him?'

Mallory arched thick brows. 'He's built quite a reputation. In just a few years. I hear he learned how to shoot from Clay Allison. Right here in Texas. He killed Curly Quentin, you know.'

'What artillery?'

'I heard it's a Colt .45, not much different from yours. They say you can't see his hand go to leather.' He was watching Bastian's face.

Bastian nodded. 'I heard he was fast.'

'That might be an understatement.'

Bastian smiled slightly. 'I'm doing this, Brett. I owe it to Jonah. And to Maggie.'

'Is that the way she looks at it?'

Bastian sighed. 'She's a woman, Brett. She's afraid.'

'I'm afraid, too.'

A heavy silence filtered into the space between them.

'You're not sure I can do it. You think I've lost my edge.'

'I wouldn't ever bet any money against you,' Mallory said soberly. 'Maybe that belly gun will give you an advantage. Or maybe you'll get the last shot in and outlast him. Remember that shoot-out we had together over in Fort Griffin? We both got hit before we could find the trigger. But when it was over, the other boys was laying on the floor with their toes pointed at the ceiling, and both of us walked away from it.'

'I remember,' Bastian said.

'Like I always told you. Accurate is better than fast.'

Bastian nodded. 'That kept me alive when I took on that assignment you insisted on me taking against my better judgment,' Bastian grinned.

'You wouldn't have met Maggie if you hadn't,' Mallory countered.

'You win,' Bastian surrendered. 'As usual. Do you have any information about where Sumner might be about now? I heard he was in Kansas.'

'I have no idea,' Mallory told him. 'I just hope that you find him, since you're determined to do this, before he kills any more innocent people.'

'That's one reason I'm here,' Bastian told him.

On that same afternoon Sumner rode into Boulder, Colorado.

He had put all thought of Bastian out of his head. In his world, you kept your mind on what was before you, not something that might or might not happen in your future. If your head got ahead of reality, it could kill you.

Boulder was a sizeable town, with hotels, saloons and banks along the main thoroughfare. Women sauntered along looking in shop windows, carrying parasols and fancy purses. Most men on the street wore suits with ties, and few were carrying iron.

Sumner rode slowly down the dusty street, looking the place over. He found himself momentarily envying these ordinary citizens milling about around him, with their very routine but unhazardous daily living, and its easy tranquillity.

Sumner had never met the town marshal here, but he elected to seek him out first to inquire about the Lakota Kid. He found the marshal's office off the main street centrally, in an impressive brick building that also contained municipal offices. The marshal's quarters were reached from a side entrance, and behind that office were holding cells.

Sumner left the tired stallion at a hitching rail outside, patted its neck, and went into the building. He found himself in a rather large front room with three desks in it, a large oak one and two smaller ones on an opposite wall. There were two middle-aged women at typewriters at the small desks, and a rather young man wearing a badge at the larger one. On a wall near his desk was a poster board with city broadheads tacked to it, and several Wanted posters.

The marshal looked up and saw Sumner standing just inside the entrance. He stared at Sumner for a moment, taking note of the Peacemaker.

'Can I help you, mister?'

Sumner came over to his desk, still looking the place over. Most lawmen's offices weren't this fancy. 'Are you the marshal here?'

'The marshal is out of town. I'm Deputy Atkins. What can I do for you?'

'I'm looking for a man, and I'm hoping you might have some information on him.'

'Oh. You're one of *them.*'

Sumner gave him a look. 'Yes. I'm one of them.'

'We handle all the crime around Boulder, mister. We don't need no help with it.'

'Then why haven't you got the Lakota Kid locked up back there?' Sumner suggested.

The deputy grinned. 'You're lucky the marshal ain't here. One of his cousins was murdered by a bounty man.'

Sumner stood there without replying.

The deputy shook his head, and got up from the desk. He came round to take a better look at Sumner. He was an inch shorter than Sumner, and had a lean, wiry look about him.

'What's your name, bounty man?'

'Sumner. Wesley Sumner.'

A grin slid off Atkins' face. 'You're Certainty Sumner?' Both women at the typewriters looked up quickly.

'Is that important?' Sumner said sourly.

'It is to me. Listen, it's pretty noisy in here. You want a cup of coffee?'

Sumner hesitated, then nodded. 'Sure.'

'Follow me,' the deputy told him.

Sumner followed him down a short corridor to a small room with a pot-belly stove against the far wall, with a coffee pot simmering on it. Atkins poured them

91

two cups and they sat down at a table across from each other.

'Now.' Atkins resumed. 'I've heard a lot about you, Sumner.'

'Most of it's bull-pucky,' Sumner said quietly.

Atkins grinned. 'Are you after the Kid?'

Sumner sipped at his coffee It tasted good after a long day on the trail. 'He has a good amount on him. That's what makes it interesting for me.'

The deputy grunted. 'At least you're honest about it. But I suspect that on some level, you got a big chip on your shoulder.'

Sumner was surprised by the comment. It seemed a little deep for the usual lawman. 'There were a couple of things that probably started me off in this direction. But I do it because it's the only thing I know. Or am good at.'

'I knew Curly Quentin,' Atkins said, sipping his coffee.

'I'll probably shoot the next man that mentions that name,' Sumner remarked with an acid look.

'I was just a kid. Playing cards in a saloon in Abilene. I was getting along fine with Quentin. Then I got a great hand and raked in a big pot. Quentin accused me of cheating. When I refused to give up the pot, he called me out. I couldn't beat him, so I wouldn't draw down on him. Just for fun then he drew and fired twice, taking this ear-lobe off and grazing the other one.' He turned his head and showed Sumner the missing lobe where his ear was all scarred up. 'He took the pot anyway, and I had to leave without it.'

'You're lucky he didn't put one between your eyes,' Sumner told him.

'You killed one nasty sonofabitch when you took him down,' Atkins said, staring past Sumner 'He had a big string of killings behind him. I didn't know that when I sat down to play poker with him.' He caught Sumner's eye. 'Did he have a big reward on him?'

'I didn't kill him for the bounty,' Sumner said. 'I didn't know about bounties then. He was hoorawing me in front of my friend Clay Allison. When I started talking back to him he called me out. I had no choice.'

'You know Clay Allison?' He was obviously impressed.

'He's a good friend. But let's get back to the Lakota Kid.'

Atkins nodded. 'Sorry. I guess I just wanted to be able to say I set with Certainty Sumner. Don't pay me no mind.'

'The Kid,' Sumner insisted.

Atkins nodded. 'He's been in this area before. Murdered a married couple on the Denver road, not far from here. Me and the marshal went down there. After a close neighbour, we was the first on the scene. It wasn't pretty. He had tied and gagged the husband and made him watch while he raped and did other things to his wife.'

Sumner was shaking his head. Memories of his own aunt being raped and murdered in front of him while he was bound, at the tender age of seventeen, came crashing into his consciousness like hot lead from a Colt.

'When he was through with the wife he cut that man's

innards right out and dumped them on the floor beside him.' He was staring past Sumner, sober-faced. 'I'd like to see that boy in hell with his back broke.'

Sumner nodded. 'That's where I'm sending him,' he stated.

'He'll want to do that to you,' Atkins added. 'When he finds out you're after him. His aim will be to take you alive. He's fast, but he'll avoid a face-down if he can. He'll have some cohorts grab you some dark night. Then he'll take you to some private place and work on you. He plays dirty little games with people. To make the whole thing more entertaining.'

'Sounds like a real likeable fellow.'

'If he thinks it's too hard to take you alive, he'll plan on back-shooting you. That's what you have to understand. There will be no fairness about it. And remember. If he learns that you're coming for him, he won't wait for you to find him. He'll come after you. And he hates bounty hunters. He brags that he's killed three of them.'

'I appreciate the heads-up,' Sumner said after a moment. 'Now. What have you heard about him lately? Did you try to find him after that stage hold-up not far from here?'

The deputy shook his head slowly. 'Those people don't know how lucky they were. Yes, we both went out looking for him. But he just disappeared from sight. I just talked to a drifter yesterday, though, who swears he saw the Kid in a little town west of here that same day.'

'Did he say the name of the place?'

'Yes, it was a burg called Smith's Crossing. A little one-horse town. He could be hiding out there, hunkering down till he does his next job. As soon as the marshal gets back, we'll probably ride over there to check it out. But he won't be back here for almost a week. He had to testify in court in Denver.'

Sumner swigged the rest of the coffee. 'Well, thanks for the coffee, and the palaver,' he said to the young deputy. He rose from his chair.

'You're going to try to beat us to him, aren't you?'

Sumner smiled at that. 'Isn't that what you want to happen?' he suggested.

Atkins coloured slightly. 'I wouldn't register any complaints if you took him down before we could locate him. Something tells me you're better at this than either of us.'

'I'll give it my best effort,' Sumner told him.

Atkins rose, too. 'I knew I'd like you. You'd do to ride the river with.'

Sumner didn't respond. Atkins walked him to the outside door, and then the bounty hunter was gone.

The village of Smith's Crossing wasn't much to look at. Sumner reined in the stallion at the near end of town, and looked the place over. It looked a lot like the tiny settlement of Pawnee Junction, where Sumner had rescued Dulcie Provost in that world that seemed like a hundred years ago now. A lot had happened in the interim, to him and probably to Dulcie. Some days he felt as if he were deluding himself in thinking she would still be waiting back there for his possible return. She was a girl who would probably want to get on with her life.

He rode slowly down the sunny street. There were a few people moving about, local townsfolk and a few cowhands. There was a saloon and a bank, and Sumner was surprised to see a small hotel at the far end of the street.

The saloons were always the social centres of these towns, and as such the best locations to find out information about current events. So Sumner reined in at the Mountain View saloon, hitched his mount outside, and took a look inside the place.

It was late morning and the saloon was almost empty. There was one patron at the long bar, talking to a slim bartender, and a table near the rear with two men drinking from a bottle of Planters Rye whiskey. The men at the table were ranch hands, and had a tough look. They looked up and stared for a moment at the newcomer, then went back to their drinking. Sumner walked over to the bar, not far from the man standing with the bartender.

'I'll take a black ale, barkeep,' Sumner said in a quiet voice.

'It will be right here,' the barman responded. He looked Sumner over, and made a motion with his eyes to alert the patron to take a look at Sumner.

The man did, and found himself staring at the hefty Peacemaker on Sumner's hip. Sumner had removed the one-shot Derringer from where he had snugged it into his right boot, as a temporary measure, and replaced it to a thin holster at the back of his belt, since that holster had been repaired. It was now well hidden from view under his dark coat, even from the back.

'You a stranger in town?' the man near Sumner spoke up to him.

Sumner regarded him diffidently. 'Just passing through,' he replied.

The bartender brought the ale and Sumner quaffed part of it. Then he spoke to the bartender. 'You ever heard of the Lakota Kid?'

The bartender laughed. 'Who hasn't?'

'I heard he was in town. Has he been in here?'

The barkeep frowned. 'Maybe. Why would you care, mister?'

Sumner was mildly irritated by his manner. 'Because I'm going to kill him,' he said deliberately.

The man beside Sumner turned to him again. 'Say. Them clothes of yours. That Colt on your hip. Would you be Certainty Sumner?'

Sumner dropped a brittle look on him. 'I'll ask again. Has either of you seen the Kid in town in the past few days?'

The bartender had a new look on his face. He swallowed hard. 'Well. He was in here.'

'How long ago?' Sumner persisted.

But before the other man could reply, one of the ranch men at the table, the taller, tougher-looking one, called out to the barkeep. 'You don't have to answer no questions from no bounty man,' he said loudly.

All three men at the bar turned to him, including Sumner.

'You a friend of the Kid?' Sumner said acidly.

'No, and I ain't no friend of bounty hunters.' He had never heard of Sumner. 'That's what you are, ain't it?'

Sumner turned back to the bar. 'Now. As we were saying.'

'Don't talk to him!' the ranch man called out again. 'We don't blow on other customers here, back-shooter!'

Sumner sighed. Maybe he had enough, anyway. He picked up his ale again.

'Matter of fact, we don't like drinking in the same place with killers for hire!' From behind Sumner again. 'Why don't you just haul your freight out of here, mister?'

The man standing near Sumner at the bar turned to the big man. 'Gus. I don't think you get it. This is Certainty Sumner.'

'What's that supposed to mean to me?'

'This is the boy that killed Curly Quentin.' In a hushed voice. Sumner sighed heavily and swigged some more ale.

'Who the hell is Curly Quentin?' Gus barked out.

That response pleased Sumner, and he smiled to himself.

'Quentin was the fastest gun in ten states and the Territory,' the bartender answered for him, in a soft voice.

But Gus's reason was impaired by the Planters Rye. He shoved his chair away from his table with his hand out over a Colt Navy revolver.

'I don't care if he killed Billy Bonney. I won't set here drinking with him. Now, will you go peaceable, bounty man?'

'For God's sake, Gus!' the man near Sumner muttered.

Sumner turned to his challenger. 'I'm here for the Kid. I don't want any other trouble. Why don't you do us both a big favour and let it go?'

'You won't get any trouble if you haul your freight out of here. Right now!'

'I haven't finished my ale yet,' Sumner replied. 'You wouldn't want me to just leave it here, would you?'

Gus was furious. 'All right, pond scum. I'm through talking.' Gus had never lost in a draw-down, and was full of confidence. 'Go for your iron!'

In the next moment Gus went for the Colt, and he was fast. But by the time he had cleared leather, Sumner's big Peacemaker was levelled directly at his heart, and Gus hadn't even seen the gun come into his hand.

Gus' thick face changed as he stared numbly at the muzzle of the Colt. Waiting for eternity. His gun slowly dropping back into its holster.

Sumner held the Peacemaker on him for another deadly moment, then twirled it backwards twice into its leather nest.

A low muttering came from the bartender.

'Gus,' Sumner said evenly, 'you must have mustard seed for brains. If you're not out of here in the next minute or so, I might re-think just what to do with you.'

Gus didn't need a second ultimatum. He ran a hand over his mouth, nodded silently to his companion, and they both left without further comment. When they were gone, Sumner turned back to the bar.

'If he hadn't been such a lame-brain, I'd have bought him a drink for not knowing who Curly Quentin was.'

They both grinned.

'Thanks for not killing Gus,' the man beside him offered. 'He always was a kind of jackass.'

Sumner swigged the rest of the ale.

'The Kid was in here, all right. He came in last night, raising hell. Had another man with him. I think he called him Dude. Seemed a little off up here, you know? I'd guess his head is empty as last year's crow's nest with the bottom punched out.'

'Nice combination,' Sumner suggested. 'A crazy man and a retard.'

The bartender leaned forwards. 'They're dangerous, Sumner. Somebody heard them talking. About robbing our general store down the street. They'll kill the owner. And he's got a sixteen-year-old daughter. You know how bad that could get. I told old Eben, but he won't leave. And we got no law in town.'

Sumner absorbed that quietly. 'I suppose this is the best place to find him. Later tonight.'

'I'm sure they'll be back in here. Maybe shooting up the place. Threatening my customers.'

Sumner nodded. 'You have any idea where he might be staying?'

'Your guess is as good as mine. I think the man he was with lives hereabouts somewhere.'

'Well. I'll be back.'

'I hope you find that sonofabitch,' the fellow beside him said. Sumner gave him a small smile. 'I always have,' he replied.

SIX

On his way out of Texas on the afternoon of that same day when Sumner was inquiring about the Lakota Kid in Colorado, Luther Bastian stopped in Medicine Bend, where Brett Mallory had sent him on that special assignment to avenge a Texas Ranger's death, a couple years ago.

It all came back to him as he rode into town on that overcast afternoon. He had come to confront the Gabriel gang, but most of them had already left, heading back into the Indian Territory. The two who had stayed over briefly were a cowardly back-shooter named Cuckoo Bobo and a lightning fast gun called Sweet Daddy, the fastest draw in five states. Bastian had taken them both down, but was wounded twice himself.

The town looked the same. It was small, but there was a saloon and a couple of stores on the main street. It was actually a rather pretty little town, with rows of white-washed clapboard buildings and houses. He rode directly to the mayor's house, a fellow named Ethan Purvis. His black stallion, looking a lot like Sumner's

101

except for the star on its muzzle and legs, he hitched outside and knocked on Purvis' door. When Purvis answered it, his expression exploded into surprise.

'My God! Luther!' He looked over the dark clothing, the attire of the Preacher. 'I don't understand. I thought you were ranching down by the border, with Maggie and Jonah.'

'I am,' Bastian said. 'I've taken on a special job, Ethan. One requiring the use of my gun again.'

'I'm sorry to hear that,' Purvis told him. 'Look, come on in and set. I see we got some talking to do.' He was silver-haired, and paunchy.

They entered the kitchen where Bastian had sat on numerous occasions before, and sat at a wide table. The mayor called his wife in and there was a pleasant reunion with her, then she excused herself to let the men talk.

'Can I get you something to drink?'

'Not now,' Bastian told him. 'How have you been, Mayor?'

'Oh, things are pretty quiet around here nowadays. Since you cleaned out the Gabriel people. Me and the missus are just fine. How does Jonah like ranching?'

'He took to it real well,' Bastian smiled. 'Maggie likes it, too. We have a good thing going down there, Ethan.'

Purvis' face lengthened. 'Then what's all this about?' Looking down at the custom Colt on his belly.

Bastian told him the whole story, about Jonah's leg, and Amos Latham and his offer. He pulled out the wanted dodger and showed it to him.

'I've heard that name,' Purvis said. 'Wasn't he in the

same business as you?'

Bastian nodded. 'And he has quite a reputation.'

'He'll give the whole profession a bad name. That's too bad.'

'It happens,' Bastian said. 'There are other bounty men that I wouldn't turn my back on.'

Purvis just sat and stared at him. 'I remember you riding in here that day when I'd never set eyes on you before. I'd taken Jonah in temporarily and I think you scared him at first. Until he found out the Rangers sent you.'

'I liked him almost on first sight,' Bastian smiled.

'The boy developed an immediate hero-worship for you,' Purvis grinned. 'He had a thing about Texas Rangers.'

'I'm glad you sent him with me to Maggie.' He paused. 'So you have no information on Sumner.'

He shook his head. 'I could check with a nearby sheriff. Did you think he was in this area?'

'I heard he was in Kansas.'

'Say, wait a minute.' He went into his office in the next room for a moment, and came back carrying a paper. 'This is a regular report the sheriff in the next county sends me because we're old friends.' He scanned the page for a moment. 'Oh, here. Some crazy boy called the Lakota Kid, that was in this area last year, has been seen up in Colorado, and held up a stage there. There's a bounty on him. And a rumor that one of you boys is after him. Somebody that dresses like a gambler.'

'Damn. That would be Sumner.' In a half-whisper.

Purvis studied his long, aquiline face. 'I'm kind of

sorry I found that.'

'Can you spare that report?'

'Sure. Take it.' Soberly.

'I appreciate this, Ethan.' Folding the paper and shoving it into a pocket. 'And I don't need anybody else worrying over me. I already have Maggie and Jonah.'

Purvis sighed. 'I know how good you are. But things can happen, Luther. And you said this boy is good too. How do you know how it will work out?'

'I don't. But like I told Maggie, I have no choice.' He smiled. 'And I'm pretty good at this, remember?'

'I always have a bad feeling about last or special projects that can make or break a man's future. Go back to your ranch, Luther. Back to Maggie and Jonah. Find some other way to fix Jonah's leg.'

'There is no other way,' Bastian told him. 'But listen. You've been a big help. I'll never forget you.'

'I could never repay you for what you did here,' Purvis said heavily. 'Look. When you get back to that ranch of yours, say hey to Maggie and Jonah for me.'

'They'll be glad to hear from you,' Bastian told him.

Later that afternoon in Smith's Crossing, while Sumner was checking into the small, rather sleazy hotel down the street, the Lakota Kid unexpectedly returned to the saloon where Sumner had been in late morning.

This time he was with another man, the one called Dude. They came in laughing and swaggering, and the bartender recognized them first.

'Oh, hell,' he muttered. He had thought they wouldn't come in until evening. The Kid and his companion took

a table not far from the front entrance, and the Kid
pounded his fist on the table.

'Hey, barkeep! Let's have some service over here! My
good friend and me are so thirsty we're spitting dust!'

The other patrons around the room all stared glumly
at the newcomers. The bartender who had spoken with
Sumner earlier sighed heavily and went over to the Kid's
table.

'What can I get you, gentlemen?'

The Kid studied him for a moment. 'Say, did I tell you
that you look just like a second cousin of mine back in
Missouri?'

Dude looked at the bartender and grinned insipidly.
'A second cousin.' He gave a reedy laugh. He was
thinner than the Kid, but looked sinewy-tough. He wore
a bowler hat and a soiled, checkered vest.

'No,' the bartender said patiently. 'You didn't tell me.'

'I killed that sonofabitch,' the Kid said.

The bartender was becoming tense. 'I'm ready to
take your order now, boys. What will you have?'

The Kid frowned. As on that day of the stage hold-up
he was wearing a bright red vest over a work shirt, and
his trousers were rawhide. He tipped a dark brown
Stetson back off his forehead.

'Ain't you interested in my cousin, flea-brain?'

The bartender was getting very tight inside. 'Look. If
you boys don't want to order, I got other customers.'

The Kid was frowning. 'I don't give a damn about the
other customers,' he growled out. 'I want you to hear
about my cousin.'

'He killed that cousin!' Dude giggled out.

'Maybe I better get on with my work,' the bartender tried again.

'You get on with your work when I say so,' the Kid told him. 'Set your freight down here a minute.' With a tough, warning look.

The bartender looked around for support, but found none. He hesitated, then sat down on an empty chair.

'Now,' the Kid said. 'Would you like to know how you remind me of my cousin?'

'You remind him of his cousin!' the companion Dude snickered. He had been recently released from prison, where he had been serving time for raping a pre-puberty girl and beating her father.

'Shut up, Dude,' the Kid said quietly.

The Kid stared at the barkeep with the cold blue stare of a born killer. 'Well?' he said pointedly.

'Huh?' Dude said belatedly. Nobody paid any attention to him.

'Sure,' the bartender replied to the Kid's question.

'You remind me of him because you're both so ugly you couldn't flag down a gut wagon.'

The bartender lowered his eyes from the hard stare. The noise in the room had simmered down to silence in just a moment. Everybody was now looking over at the Kid's table.

'That boy's looks got in my craw so bad I shot him,' the Kid added. 'And you got that same look.' He moved his hand out over the Dardick 1500 on his belt.

'Whatever you say, Kid. I can't argue with artillery.'

'Why don't you let him get back at it, Kid?' a tough-looking drinker at the bar called over. 'We're getting thirsty over here.'

The Kid glared at him. 'You want to get in on this, cow prodder?'

'Let me take him, Kid,' Dude suggested breathlessly, worked up by all the palaver.

'I think you got all the trouble you can handle already,' the ranch hand said more to himself than to the Kid.

The Kid's face fell into scowl lines. 'Get back behind that bar before I shoot you,' he said to the bartender. The barkeep rose gratefully and hurried back behind the bar. Then the Kid rose from the table and walked over to the fellow who had spoken to him.

'What the hell did you mean by that? About me having trouble?' In a low, menacing tone.

The other man faced him. Now you could hear a pin drop in the big room. 'I'm just saying what everybody already knows. Certainty Sumner is in town. And he's looking for you.'

The Kid's whole manner changed. 'How do you know that?'

A shrug. 'He was in here earlier. He knows you're here.' Then he went too far. 'You might have just a few hours left to you.'

The Kid's face crimsoned slightly, and his breath came shorter. But he controlled himself. 'Is that what you think?'

'Well. I wouldn't want him after me. Every man he ever went after is in Boot Hill pushing up daisies now. He's very efficient.'

The Kid's words came out tight, like paste from a

tube. 'You know a lot about Sumner, pea-brain.'

'I know he'll probably kill you when he finds you. If I was you, I'd be thinking of riding out of Smith's Crossing.'

'Oh, is that what you'd do?'

'No offence.'

'No, it's all right. I appreciate the warning. If it wasn't for good citizens like yourself, I might have been dead years ago.'

'Well,' the other man said quizzically.

'That was a lot of advice you gave me,' the Kid said.

He turned back to the table, but after a few steps he whirled back, drew the Dardick, and fired off two well-aimed shots, the gun roaring in the confines of the room. The ranch hand screamed out in sudden pain, with both of his knee-caps shattered by the hot lead.

There were hushed mutterings around the room, but no one dared to interfere. The ugly-looking Dude was on his feet, too, and was aiming his old weapon at the shot man, to finish him off.

'No,' the Kid ordered him. 'This is better.'

The shot man had fallen to the floor and nobody went to him. He was groaning and holding a leg.

'Anybody else want to talk about Certainty Sumner?' the Kid taunted the room. There was no response.

'Come on, Dude. I don't want a drink this bad.'

They left the saloon in silence then, except for the moaning of the shot man on the floor.

Outside on the street the Lakota Kid went and leaned on his mount, thoughts flying through his head. Trying to recall stories he had heard about Certainty Sumner. Understanding that no outlaw wanted to hear that Sumner had picked up a dodger on him. He was known to be relentless in his pursuit. He had never given up on a man. And he came to kill. It was him or you. There were no words that could deter him. No argument could be offered. He was very much like the Preacher of a few years back.

'What are you going to do?' Dude asked him as they stood there in the growing dusk. 'We can take him together, can't we?'

The Kid gave him a look. 'If you want to face Sumner down, have at it. There's no way I'd meet him face to face. I got much better ideas.'

Dude frowned a rheumy frown. 'Well, I'm with you, Kid.'

'The way to take Sumner down is to outsmart him. Hide in cover and just back-shoot him. That means I don't wait for him to find me. I'll make it happen my way. On my terms. Then I won't be looking over my shoulder for the next year.'

'How do we do that?'

'Just follow me,' the Kid told him, suddenly wishing he had someone with him who had some skill with a gun.

They walked their mounts down to the nearby hotel, where the Kid figured Sumner might be registered. They found a desk clerk reading a Denver newspaper behind the long desk. The place was very ordinary, with an odour of cooking coming from a back room. No pictures on the walls, no carpet on the weathered floor.

The clerk wore a green visor and had a wart on his left cheek. He looked up from the paper and frowned slightly when he saw the Kid.

'Gentlemen. Can I rent you a nice room for the night? We have clean sheets and charge a dollar for a bath.'

'We're looking for a friend,' the Kid said.

'Yeah, a friend.' From Dude, beside him.

The Kid gave him a look. 'His name is Sumner,' he went on. 'He might have checked in here yesterday.'

'We have a strict policy, boys. We keep the identity of our guests as private as we can.'

The Kid laughed in his throat. 'In this flea-bag?'

The clerk looked hurt. 'But I can give you two nice rooms, if you'd like. Or one bigger room with two beds. Your choice.' A tight smile.

The Kid drew his revolver and placed it gently on the bridge of the clerk's nose. 'Now, I'll ask you one more time. And if you give me any more trouble I'll blow your nose out through the back of your pin head.'

The clerk's eyes saucered. 'Hey! Be careful with that!'

'Is a man named Sumner registered here?'

'No, sir.'

'Anybody with dark clothes? Fancy vest? Peacemaker?'

'Why, a Mr Smith registered that might fit that description.'

'What room is he in?'

The clerk licked suddenly dry lips. 'I think it's 203. But he isn't there now.'

'Do you know where he went?'

'I think he mentioned checking on his horse. At the hostelry.'

The Kid holstered the Dardick. 'I'll bet that was easier than you thought.'

Then he backhanded the clerk across the face, knocking him against the wall behind him.

'Jesus!' the clerk gasped.

'I'm the Lakota Kid. Don't ever get crossways of me again.'

The clerk nodded, holding his cheek. 'Yes, sir.'

'Don't get crossways of the Kid,' the messy-looking Dude grinned.

The Kid gave him a scouring look. 'Shut up and come with me.'

It was just a few minutes later that the two of them arrived at the old barn-like building that housed the hostelry. The place was unlit, the hostler gone for the night. It was getting dark now, and the interior of the place was in shadow.

The Kid stopped a short distance from the building. He took a deep breath in, and felt dampness in his palms. He knew he was embarking on something that few other men had ever done. By going after Sumner before Sumner found him.

It was audacious. It was very dangerous. But it might just save his life.

'Why did you stop?' the retarded Dude wondered.

The Kid ran a hand over his mouth. 'I heard something in there. I think he's here.'

'Good. Let's go in and take him.' Eagerly.

The Kid grabbed him by his shirt. 'Listen to me,

111

dummy. He has to be facing away from us. If not we walk on past and hope he doesn't recognize me. If he's busy with his horse we'll move up on him. Did you take them spurs off?'

Dude nodded. 'Like you told me.'

'There will be no talking. No scraping of feet on gravel. Don't even breathe till he's down. At my signal, we'll both unload on him. You got all of that?'

'Sure,' the other man replied quickly.

The Kid gave him a sour look, and took a deep breath in. 'All right. Let's go do it.'

They moved up slowly and noiselessly to the big yawning entrance to the hostelry. When they got there, the Kid stopped again. Down the aisle between stalls was a dark figure. Rather tall, slim, and a bulge at his jacket where a Peacemaker would be. The Kid's mouth went dry as old newspaper.

Both of their guns were out. The Kid moved a few paces forward, with Dude following. They were fifteen feet away. The Kid didn't think he could afford to try for closer. He nodded to his scared partner, and they both levelled their weapons at the back of the man cleaning a curry brush beside a stall.

But at that moment, the dark figure turned and looked directly at them. The Kid held his hand up for Dude to abort.

'Can I help you gentlemen?' the voice came to them.

The voice was of an old man. He had white eyebrows and a long nose. There was also a white mustache.

The Kid just stared for a moment.

'Who's that?' Dude asked inanely.

The Kid ignored him. He walked on over to the older fellow, and looked him over. 'For Christ's sake,' he muttered.

'Is something wrong, bub?' the old man asked.

The Kid angrily shoved the Dardick into its holster. 'Who the hell are you?'

'The name is Peters. I'm here to curry-comb my animal. Who are you?'

'Hell,' Dude was grumbling.

'I'm somebody you don't want to know, old-timer. We're looking for a man. Was somebody else in here just before we came?'

'Why, now that you mention it, there was a man.'

'What did he look like?'

'Yes, what did he look like?' Dude echoed him.

The Kid turned to him red-faced. 'Shut up!' he fairly screamed into Dude's face.

Dude stepped away from him a half-step. 'Sorry, Kid.'

'Now,' the Kid repeated. 'What did this man look like?'

The old fellow shrugged, a little intimidated by the Kid now. 'Well. He was tall. Dark clothes. Wore this big Peacemaker on a gunbelt.'

'Sonofabitch!' the Kid muttered. 'We just missed him.'

'A friend of yours?' the older man said.

The Kid focused on him fiercely. 'So he left here walking?'

'Oh, no. He took his horse out. Saddled up and rode off.'

The Kid stared hard at him. 'Rode off?'

113

'Yes, sir.'

'You're sure about that?'

'Oh, yes. Gave me a smile when he left.' Watching the Kid's face.

The Kid looked over at Dude. 'That bastard changed his mind! He's scared of me!'

'You think so?' With irritating incredulity.

'You know which way he rode off to?' the Kid went on, ignoring Dude.

Another shrug. 'How should I know?'

Unknown to any of them, even though Sumner had taken the stallion out, it was just to test the strength of a new shoe on the horse's forefoot. He would return within the hour. But the Kid had no way of knowing that. He took his gun out and slugged the old fellow with it.

The old man called Peters slammed against the door of his horse's stall, and slid to the ground, dazed and bleeding from his right ear. When he looked up, he saw the Kid's revolver aimed at his head. He was gasping in pain.

'Now. Try to remember,' the Kid grated out.

Peters had no idea. 'Yes, I think I remember now. He was heading east,' he lied.

'That's more like it. I should shoot you for lying to me. But this is your lucky night. I'm in a good mood now.' He turned to Dude. 'This is a good luck omen. I'm not staying in this rat-hole tonight. I'm riding west just as fast as my mount will carry me.'

'West?'

'That's right. Now, if you're coming with me, let's

114

saddle up and ride.'

'I'm ready!' the inept cohort grinned wildly.

It was not much later that evening when the misguided Luther Bastian arrived in a border town in southern Colorado not far south of Smith's Crossing. It was rather quiet along the main street as he rode down to the only saloon, rail-hitched his horse, and went inside to ask about Sumner. After speaking with the bartender and another man and learning nothing, he walked on down the street to Ned's Pool Hall and Gambling Parlour to have boiled eggs and beer before finding accommodation for the night.

Bastian took a table near the counter where the owner dealt with customers for use of the two pool tables situated in the centre of the room, and to take orders for light meals. There was a man alone at another table not far away, and two other customers playing pool at the closest pool table. The owner came and took Bastian's order. He looked him over carefully, noting the dark clothing and the custom Colt that lay across Bastian's belly, in full view.

'Can't I talk you into a game before you eat?' the owner asked quietly. 'There's a boy over there that would join you, and a table is free.'

'No thanks,' Bastian replied. 'I just want to get myself a bed for the night. Is that boarding house down the street bug and rat free?'

'Oh, yes, sir. That's run by a personal friend of mine.' He was still looking Bastian over. 'Say, have you been in here before?'

115

Bastian gave him a sober look. 'Can't say I have.'

The owner nodded and left. Before returning behind the counter, he stopped at the pool table where the two men were playing, and said something in low tones to the nearest player, a rather big, tough-looking man with a broken nose and pock-marked face. As the owner moved on to get Bastian's order, the big man spoke to his companion and they both looked over at Bastian.

Bastian wasn't paying any attention. He was wondering how close he was to Sumner at that moment, and how a confrontation with him might turn out. He knew he could not afford to lose in a face-down. That would leave Maggie and Jonah alone at the ranch. Without the one who had brought them there.

His justification for taking such a risk was that, as he undertook this quest, Jonah was in the process of getting his leg made right by a good doctor. No matter what happened here, that would be accomplished.

'Hey! You over there!'

The big man at the pool table had called out to Bastian. Bastian looked up at him and did not respond.

'You're the Preacher, ain't you?'

Bastian sighed. He looked over at the owner, who was occupied behind the counter. 'How's that order coming?'

The owner turned to him, then shot a glance at the big man. 'Oh, it's almost ready. Did you say beer or ale?'

'Beer,' Bastian said sourly. 'And the eggs.'

'Say, mister. Maybe you didn't hear me,' the big fellow called over again. 'You look like the Preacher. Am I right?'

116

Bastian shook his head slowly. 'I'm Luther Bastian. If that helps you any.'

The big fellow gestured toward his companion. 'See this boy here? He's a nephew of Simon Gabriel. The man you murdered in cold blood a couple years ago.'

'Simon was my uncle,' the younger man put in. He was slimmer than his comrade, with a bony face and long, yellowish hair under a Stetson. He was sober-faced and spoke more softly than the other man. They both carried sidearms.

'Sorry to hear that,' Bastian told him. 'Your uncle was a stone killer and wanted for murder. He was killed in a fair face-down and the world is better off without him.'

Gabriel had been the outlaw that Brett Mallory had sent him after, when one of Gabriel's gang had killed a Texas Ranger. On that assignment he had met both Maggie and Jonah.

The Gabriel nephew laid his pool cue on the table and stepped away from it. 'Nobody calls my uncle a killer!' he said tightly.

The big man put a hand on his arm, and stepped in front of him. Obviously the experienced gunman of the two. 'The boy is right, Preacher,' he growled out now. He was considered good with his old Colt, locally. 'And it's been years since you did your murderous work, ain't it? You might not be as good as you was then.'

'Do you really want to find out?' Bastian said pleasantly.

The way he said it, and the look of the special Peacemaker on Bastian's belly, made the challenger less certain of what he was heading into. He hesitated before making a reply. 'Gabriel's death has to be answered.'

The owner was now standing at the end of the counter with Bastian's eggs and beer, but frozen in place. 'Maybe you should take this outside, boys. What do you think?' The lone man at the other table rose quietly and left.

Everybody ignored both of them.

Bastian turned from the pool table to the owner. Making no move to respond to the big man. 'Bring that over here. I'm hungry.'

The big fellow and the nephew exchanged a look. And the big man secretly felt a sense of relief. The owner carefully brought Bastian's order over and set it in front of him with a quizzical look, then hurried away.

Bastian swigged some beer, and picked up an egg. 'Look. I got more important things on my mind than jawing with the likes of you two. So I'm going to do you both a big favour tonight. I'm not going to kill you.'

The big man just stood there for a moment. Still looking at the ominous Peacemaker that looked like a cannon on Bastian's gunbelt. He knew now he had gone too far, and Bastian had given him a way to save face. He decided he would take it.

'So you're refusing to face down.'

'I'm refusing to kill you,' Bastian repeated, taking a bite of the egg. 'Why don't you just let it lay?'

The big man hadn't gotten out of it gracefully yet. 'You should apologize to this boy for shooting his uncle. However it went down.'

Bastian swallowed the bite. 'I'm not sorry I took him down. But I'm sorry you happen to be related to him, kid. That's bad luck. The good luck is, if you leave here without giving me any more trouble, you'll live through this day.'

'Well,' the big man said to the nephew. 'I guess that's enough. Come on, boy. I don't want to play pool with your uncle's killer setting there. Let's call it a night.'

The younger man shrugged. Disappointed. 'Hell. All right.'

They put their cue sticks down, went over and paid the owner, and came past Bastian's table.

'I wouldn't come in here no more, Preacher. This boy's got friends in this town that might not be as nice as we are.'

Bastian looked up and gave him a look that made him wish he had gone on out. 'If I ever come in here again, you better hope you're not here. I might not be in such a good mood.'

The big fellow decided it was the better part of judgment not to reply. The two left without further comment.

Bastian ate and drank in peace then, and when he was finished, he decided to take a long shot and ask about Sumner. He called the owner over, who seemed disappointed that there hadn't been a shoot-out.

'I'm looking for a wanted man. A bounty hunter called Sumner. Has he been in this area lately?'

The owner frowned. 'You talking about the one called Certainty Sumner?' Bastian nodded. 'That's what they call him.'

'Why, he ain't got no bounty on him. Not from around here, anyway.'

'This one isn't from around here. Has he been through here?'

The owner hesitated. 'Well. Some boy that drifted through here earlier said he saw Sumner up in Smith's Crossroads. Might have been after a low-life called the Lakota Kid.'

'He's still hunting bounties?'

'That's what I hear.'

Bastian absorbed that silently. Then: 'I'm surprised.'

'You mean you're going after Sumner?'

'That's my plan.'

'When you find him, what do you intend to do with him?' He didn't know Bastian's reputation.

Bastian looked up at him with a smile. 'I won't have a choice. He would never be taken in. I'll have to kill him, of course.'

He threw some coins on to the table, and a moment later was gone.

SEVEN

The mood was sombre at the Provost ranch. Dulcie was keeping to herself a lot, and not volunteering for as many tasks around the house and the range. At the traditional formal dinner meal, she sometimes appeared in work clothes, and rarely initiated a conversation with her father or Jake Cahill, who usually ate with them.

To add to her low mood, she had overheard a couple of bunkhouse cowboys offer their opinion that Certainty Sumner was obviously dead. So on a bright morning in early summer, a couple of days after Bastian's arrival in the small Colorado town in his pursuit of Sumner, Maynard Provost found his daughter out mending fences a half-mile from the house, and suggested they ride into town together to hopefully brighten her day.

'We could pick out some gingham cloth for a new dress, and give our seamstress a job she needs.'

She turned to him soberly. She was wearing work clothes, but looked very feminine in them, showing a lot of curves. Her auburn hair was in a twist behind her head, and she was wearing a modest-brim Stetson, but despite the unintended camouflage, she looked like she could make a man's breath come short with just a glance at her.

She made a face, and still looked pretty. 'I think I'd rather be outside, Papa.'

'You will be outside. It's a nice long ride into town. I'm taking the buggy, and I want you to keep me company.'

She gave him a look. 'I know what you're doing. I'll be all right.'

'Thinking about it all the time is like watching a pot boil,' he told her. 'Time begins to stand still. Come on, I need this too.'

Dulcie reluctantly nodded, and less than an hour later they were on their way into Ogallala. When they arrived in town, it was bustling with carriage, wagon and pedestrian traffic. Looking around, Dulcie decided her father was right. Getting out into the bigger world lightened her inside and got her mind off Sumner for a while.

They reined in at a general store and went in to look over the goods offered for sale. They were met by a rather young, slim clerk who stared at Dulcie as if he were viewing a beautiful sunset. He had never seen Provost's daughter before.

'Good morning, folks,' he managed after tearing his eyes off Dulcie. 'How can I help you on this great summer day?' Dulcie had changed into a lovely lemon-hued dress that showed off her stunning figure at its best.

'We want to see some of your gingham bolts,' Provost

told him. 'We're thinking of making my daughter here a dress.'

The clerk had regained his composure. 'My goodness, Mr Provost. Is this your daughter?'

Provost narrowed his eyes on him, as Dulcie turned her head away. 'Yes, she is. She thought she might be ready to add to her wardrobe.'

The clerk was staring again. 'Well, I must say. Anything you would put on her would beautify it!' Looking at Dulcie, hoping for a response. 'It's a rare pleasure to meet you, Miss Provost.'

Dulcie tried a weak smile.

'Now,' Provost continued. 'The gingham?'

'Oh. Of course.'

A couple of moments later they were looking the cloth over, and Dulcie liked it, and Provost ordered a long bolt of it wrapped up.

'Anything special I can get you, Miss Provost?' the clerk said in a flirting way. Dulcie shook her head, then turned to Provost. 'I think I'll wait outside, Papa. You have to pick out a saddle blanket, so I'll get some fresh air.'

'I'll be right out, honey,' Provost told her.

Dulcie went outside to get away from the clerk. She leaned against the building wall beside the door and began remembering a similar situation when she waited for Sumner to buy provisions for them when they were trying to outrun Duke Latham on their flight back to Nebraska.

As she stood there, three men came past from a saloon down the street, and as they approached, the tallest of them nudged the fellow nearest him.

'Holy Jesus! You ever see anything like that?'

In a low tone. 'Not in Ogallala.'

'Or anywhere,' the third man added.

'I'd give a thousand dollars to see that without the dress,' the second man said in a hushed tone.

They walked up near Dulcie and stopped. She glanced at them diffidently and went back to her thoughts.

'Hey, sweetheart! What are you doing out here all by yourself? Would you like some company?'

It was the tall man, who was bolder than his comrades. He had come up in front of her, and she could see he had been drinking. The other two now stood just behind him, staring hard at her figure in the dress.

'I'm not by myself,' she said soberly. 'Why don't you take your drunken friends and go sober up somewhere?'

The tall man was not deterred. He was lanky, wearing a soiled vest and a three-day growth of beard. He frowned. 'Hey. That ain't friendly.' He was looking her over hungrily. 'I just thought we might talk a little. I can get rid of these two. I'll buy you a drink down the street.'

Dulcie shook her head slowly. 'If Wesley were here, you'd be running for your lives.'

'Who?'

Dulcie took pleasure in reciting his name. 'Wesley Sumner.'

The second man who had spoken before gasped slightly. 'Who did she say?'

The tall man shrugged. 'I don't know. Somebody

named Sumner. Look. Why don't you two go get your-selves another beer? I think this sweetheart kind of likes me.'

'No, wait.' It was the third man. 'Listen, miss. Are you saying you're the girl friend of Certainty Sumner?'

Dulcie smiled at that, and felt a swelling of pride inside her. 'Yes. I am.'

Now the tall man finally got it. 'Certainty Sumner. Oh, my God!'

Dulcie smiled a beautiful, wide smile. She couldn't believe the power of his name even without his presence. 'And he wouldn't like this at all,' she commented drily.

'No, ma'am,' the tall man said in a hushed tone. 'Look, you'll have to excuse our brashness. You're right, we're drunk and don't know no better.'

'Then I'd appreciate if you'd go on your way,' Dulcie said smugly.

They all nodded. Then, as they turned to go on down the street, the tall fellow stopped for one last remark. 'Listen, there won't be no need to mention this to Sumner. Right, ma'am?'

Just then Provost emerged from the store carrying packages. He looked at the departing men with a frown. Dulcie was just replying to the tall man.

'You'll be all right. Just go on now.'

Provost came over to her as they disappeared down the street. 'What was that all about?'

'Just a few no-goods wanting a little fun,' she responded. 'But Wesley took care of the situation.'

Provost gave her a quizzical look.

'I'll tell you on the way home,' she smiled at him.

*

That evening at the ranch Dulcie felt just a little better. Having Sumner's name mentioned out on the street like that, and the fear it produced in those dislikeable men, made him seem real again to her, and illogically raised her hopes that he was still alive out there somewhere, planning to return to her as he had promised, almost a year ago.

All of Dulcie's thoughts about her future revolved around that promise. It was almost as if her future didn't exist out there without Sumner in it.

After their evening meal, Provost asked Dulcie to sit with him in his study. It was a cool night, and their housekeeper had lit a low fire in a big fireplace and they were now sitting next to it in soft chairs. On the way home, after she had told him about the three men and their reaction to Wesley Sumner's name, they hadn't mentioned the incident again. But now Provost brought it up as they sat before the fire.

'I saw you smile when you told me about the way they took mention of Sumner's name.'

She smiled again for him. 'I like it when men like that show fear of him,' she admitted. 'Even when he's a thousand miles away.'

Provost returned the smile. 'I understand.'

'I've never met a man like him, Papa. I think I never will.'

'You have deep feelings for him, don't you?'

Her green eyes met his. 'I'll never love another man.'

He sighed. 'You're pretty young to make a statement

126

like that.'

Dulcie looked into the fire. 'I mean it, Papa. I have this feeling inside me. Whenever he's near me. I can't help it. It just happens.'

Provost sighed. 'I been looking into that story that Walters fellow brought us. About some bounty man going after Sumner because of a reward out for him.'

'That couldn't possibly be true!' she retorted.

He leaned forward and clasped thick hands before him. 'One of my men just come back from the Wichita stockyards. He met a man there who has a friend that knows the father of Duke Latham.'

Dulcie frowned. Just the mention of Latham's name irritated her. 'I don't want to hear it, Papa.'

'No, wait. This may be important to us. This fellow says that it was this Amos Latham that got the fellow called the Preacher to go after Sumner. Brought a Wanted dodger to him with Sumner's name on it. And added his own cash to make it appealing to the Preacher.'

'Any lawman that would put a dodger out on Wesley must be a fool!' Dulcie exclaimed heatedly.

'Well, that's just it. This fellow said that this Amos Latham is the type that might know somebody that could make up a dodger, you know, that had no backing to it.'

Dulcie's face brightened. 'Of course! Why couldn't he do that? If he wanted revenge for Duke's death?'

'That was just a wild guess, Dulcie. He had no proof of that.'

'I don't need any proof. It makes sense. Whatever

127

that paper says Wesley did, it's wrong. He's the most upright man I've ever met.'

'I agree,' Provost told her.

Her face fell into sombre lines. 'Papa! He has a killer after him on false information! What can we do to stop this?'

Provost shook his head. 'There's no way to warn Sumner. The Preacher will get to him a lot faster than we could.'

Before she could respond to that, there was a light tapping at the open doorway and his foreman Jake Cahill stood there. 'Excuse me, folks.'

'Come on in, Jake,' Provost said heavily. 'We were just having a quiet talk.'

'Sorry to interrupt.' He looked at Dulcie with a slight frown. 'Hi, Dulcie. I heard you had a little incident in town.'

Dulcie regarded him distractedly. 'It was nothing, Jake.'

'I just wanted to mention that I was there after you, and heard something of interest. I was going to come to Maynard first, but since you're here.' Looking over at Dulcie.

Provost gave him a curious look. 'What is it, Jake?'

Cahill had removed his hat and was fingering it restlessly as he spoke. 'I talked to a man at the saloon. He had just ridden over from Denver.'

He seemed reluctant to continue.

'Go on,' Provost said warily, glancing at his daughter.

'Well. This man said there's a story floating around. About our friend Sumner.'

Dulcie's heart lurched in her chest. 'Oh, God,' she murmured. Cahill took a deep breath in, and avoided Dulcie's eyes.

'The story is that this fellow called Bastian has killed Sumner in a shoot-out.' Now he looked quickly at Dulcie.

Dulcie and Provost rose at the same time, staring hard at Cahill. Dulcie's knees felt suddenly weak, and she looked faint for a moment. Her breath was coming in shallow gasps. Provost saw her distress and came over to her and eased her back on to the chair.

Cahill went on quietly. 'This man is usually a good source. But listen, Dulcie. This could all be rumour. You know how stories get blown up. But I figured you and Maynard ought to know about it.'

Provost was standing over Dulcie, his hand on her shoulder. 'Can I get you something, honey?'

Dulcie looked up at him as if she didn't recognize him for a moment. 'What?'

'I'll have Emma bring you a cloth.'

Dulcie shook her head. Her lovely eyes now filled with tears. 'It can't be. I'd know if something happened to him.' But there was no certainty in her broken voice.

'I believe that,' Provost lied to her.

Dulcie rose again, and was able to stand steadily. 'I think I'll go look at the moon. It kept us company when we were on the trail together.'

'That's a good idea, honey,' Provost managed.

Then Dulcie left the room quietly, with both men staring after her.

*

As Jake Cahill had surmised, however, the story about Certainty Sumner's early demise was premature. Bastian hadn't found Sumner yet, but he was getting close. He inquired in Smith's Crossing that evening, and learned that Sumner had ridden out in the direction of Birney Pass, the next town west of Smith's Crossing, because he calculated that was where he might find the Lakota Kid, having just missed him at this locality.

In Birney Pass that evening, the Kid was in a good mood. He felt he had shed Sumner nicely, and might not even hear from him again. Sumner had seemingly given up on the Kid, and that was cause for celebration.

In the Last Chance saloon, therefore, the Kid was having himself a wild night. The hanger-on Dude was still with him, figuring if he stayed with the Kid a while, they would do some jobs together and Dude would end up with a pocketful of cash to spend on drinks and women.

They had just entered the saloon, taken a table near the door, and ordered a bottle of Red Top Rye brought to them. They were now swigging the drinks and laughing at the Kid's questionable jokes. Everybody around them ignored them as if they weren't there, and that began to erode the Kid's party mood. A man at a nearby table looked over at him soberly, and the Kid noticed it.

'Hey, you! You don't look like you're having any fun over there! Qué Diablo! You want a taste of our Red Top?'

The other man was sitting with two other men, and they all looked like town folk out for a quiet evening.

'No, thanks,' the other man responded. 'I'll stick with

130

my beer.'

'He'll stick with his beer,' Dude giggled, swigging some whiskey.

Nobody even looked at him.

'Beer!' the Kid frowned. 'Hell, beer is for crib babies and accountants! Which one are you, mister?'

The other men were exchanging dark glances. 'You drink your rye and we'll drink our beer,' the accosted one answered.

'He don't like your whiskey!' Dude yelled out, clapping his thigh.

'Shut up, clabber brain,' the Kid growled out through a plastered-on grin.

'Sorry.' In a muffled tone.

'Listen,' the Kid continued with the other table. 'If you won't drink with us, how about a little six-gun competition?' He drew the Dardick and several tables fell silent around him.

The bartender stopped cleaning the mahogany bar and glanced over at the Kid warily.

The Kid was waving the pistol around haphazardly now. 'You see that kerosene lamp in the back corner there, mister? I'll bet you our next drink I can put it out before you. What do you say?'

'Wait a minute there!' the bartender called over. 'There won't be no shooting inside, boys. Take it out on the street.' He had no idea who the Kid was.

The Kid frowned, aimed the Dardick at an ale bottle on the shelf just over the barkeep's shoulder, and fired. The explosion made ears ring around the room, and the bottle shattered in a hundred pieces, spraying the

131

bartender with glass and liquid.

He jumped in surprise, then looked down at the sudden mess on his arms and clothing. 'What the hell!' he muttered.

The Kid was laughing hilariously, and Dude joined in with a high giggle. But remembering the Kid's warning to him, did not venture to comment.

'Now, as I was saying,' the Kid resumed his patter with the man at the next table.

'I'm not carrying,' the other man said quietly. 'I can't play your game.'

The Kid frowned slightly. 'Oh.' He looked over at Dude. 'Give him your gun.'

'Huh?'

'Give him your goddam Colt!' the Kid yelled at him.

Dude looked down at his sidearm as if he hadn't known it was there. 'Give him my gun?'

The Kid trained the Dardick on Dude. 'Give him the Colt or I'll blow your left kidney out and have it for breakfast tomorrow.'

Dude swallowed hard, and nodded. 'Jesus. OK, Kid. Whatever you say.'

Now the entire saloon had fallen silent, watching this drama unfold. Dude got up, drew the old Colt, and delivered it to the stranger at the other table. Then he came back and sat down, watching the Kid's face.

'I don't want to play your game,' the other man said uncertainly. 'I'm no good with a gun.'

His companions watched the Kid silently.

'Please, gentlemen,' the bartender pleaded, wiping himself off with a bar cloth.

'Oh, you're probably better than you think,' the Kid grinned. 'Look, I'll show you how.'

In the next moment the Dardick roared out again, and the lamp chimney was shattered loudly, but the lamp remained lighted. The bartender shook his head. The shot had been fired just over the heads of the men at the next table, and a smaller man had ducked down. He now popped up from his chair, knocking it over. 'I'm getting out of here.' And he hurried past the Kid's table and on out through the swinging doors.

The Kid was laughing jovially again. 'That boy looked as skittery as a cow in with a herd of young bulls!' He turned back to his appointed victim. 'Well. The lamp is still burning, mister. You got a chance to beat me. Just shoot the flame out.'

'I'd rather not,' the fellow replied. 'We've decided to join our friend outside.'

He and his last friend started to rise, but the Kid stopped them. 'Hold it right there.' The grin gone from his swarthy face. Unlike Dude, he dressed well. Silver buttons on hat band. Bright red vest. The other man studied that look now and found himself wondering who this gunslinger was.

As if reading his mind, the Kid said, 'I'm the Lakota Kid. And when I say you shoot with me, you don't get up and leave.' His gun was now aimed at the other man.

The twosome slowly resumed their seats, exchanging a dark look. 'You're the Lakota Kid?'

The Kid grinned proudly. 'Now. Take a shot at that lamp. Or I'll take one at you.'

The other man looked at Dude's gun, and slowly

picked it up, hoping now that he lived through this. But at that moment, a drifter came through the door and walked over to the bar. Then he looked over at the Kid.

'Say. Ain't you the Lakota Kid?'

The Kid frowned heavily at him. He didn't like his games interrupted. 'What if I am, saddle bum?'

The drifter hesitated after that response, but then answered. 'I was just down at the hotel down the street. There was a man there asking about you.'

'What the hell are you talking about?'

'Somebody was asking about you, Kid,' Dude explained to him.

Luckily, the Kid ignored him. The drifter had turned to order a beer, and the Kid's attention was completely on him.

'You! I asked you a question! Who was asking about me?'

The man at the bar turned casually as he spoke. 'Some fellow named Sumner, I think.'

The Kid dropped the Dardick to his side, as his blocky face changed.

'Sumner? Did you say Sumner?'

'That's what I remember.'

'Did he say, Certainty Sumner?' The room was deadly quiet now.

The drifter frowned slightly. 'Why, yes. I think that was it. Say, he's a gunslinger, ain't he? Like you? He a friend of yours?'

'It's Sumner,' Dude said in a whisper.

'That ain't possible,' the Kid muttered, holstering the gun. 'Holy Jesus! That ain't possible!'

134

Then, without speaking again to anyone, the Kid slammed his hand on to the table, rose from his chair as if in a daze, and stormed out of the saloon, busting a slat in the doors as he left.

The deflated Dude followed silently.

EIGHT

That same evening at his Victorian home in Missoula, Amos Latham was a frustrated man.

He had hoped that Luther Bastian would keep him informed of his progress in his quest for Sumner, but that hadn't happened. The only news he could obtain was from his own sources, and they were few.

He hadn't known it would take this long. He watched newspapers regularly, and talked to lawmen who kept up on these things. One of them told him frankly he could not believe that Sumner had a reward out on him, and Amos had left there quickly, before further investigation could be made.

He was sitting before a small fire in his fireplace that evening, mulling all of that, when Guthrie came in from outside. Guthrie was living with Amos now, since they had taken up this mission together. Also, Amos wasn't feeling so well of late, with bouts of stomach disorder and chest pain, and Guthrie was acting as a kind of aide even though Amos had a housekeeper.

'Oh. There you are,' Guthrie greeted him. 'I thought

you'd gone upstairs to rest.'

'I can't rest. I won't ever rest till that Preacher does the job I sent him on. Hell, where is he, anyway? For all I know, he's back at his ranch spending my money on cattle, or that pretty wife of his.'

Guthrie observed him sombrely. 'He's spending that money on his boy, Amos. I believe him.'

'Well, I ain't seen a penny of return on my investment in him.' He coughed raggedly for a moment. 'I want you to find out about this, Guthrie. You owe me.'

Guthrie sighed quietly. 'You don't look so good. Are you sure you don't want to call it quits for the day?'

'I'll decide when I'm ready for bed,' Amos said garrulously. 'When I'm asleep, I don't know what's going on. Nothing gets done around here if I don't do it.'

'So you're not taking them sleeping pills the doc gave you?'

'Hell, no. That bastard is trying to make me a goddam addict! I threw them out.'

Guthrie sat down across from him on a long sofa. 'Amos, I heard something in town today I think you ought to be made aware of.'

'I hear a lot of things in town.'

'This is different. A man was at the saloon. A Bible drummer. He travels all over the country. And he run into a man that was a brother to one of Duke's friends. His name was Sloan. He said his brother had a different story about Duke than you've been told.'

Amos narrowed his eyes down on Guthrie. 'What the hell are you saying?'

Guthrie looked at his folded hands. 'This fellow said

his brother and Duke was into robbing banks and stages. With a third man named Weeks.'

'Duke? Rob banks? Sounds like bull-pucky to me. I know that Duke was kind of wild growing up. He run off from home early. While his mother was alive, he'd write her once a year to say he was doing great. There wasn't never no hint that he was in trouble with the law.'

'Well, that's not all of it. Sloan's brother says that Duke got into it with that rancher he was working for, and got fired. Then, to get back on the rancher, Duke took his daughter. She didn't run away.'

'What?'

'The story is that Duke intended to keep her, and that he . . . well, he beat on her, Amos. He was going to marry her against her will, but the rancher hired a bounty hunter to go after her and bring her back.'

He had finally gotten Amos' full attention. Amos stared across at him with a straight-lined look. 'You mean. . . ?'

Guthrie nodded. 'Certainty Sumner.'

Amos' eyes widened slightly. 'Sonofabitch.'

'Sloan's story is that Duke and his men were shot down in fair fights with Sumner, when he tried to rescue the girl. Dulcie, as I remember.'

Amos Latham's head was spinning from all that.

'This is just one man's version of events,' Guthrie went on. 'But I have to be honest with you, Amos. It had a ring of truth to it.'

Amos sat forward on his chair, his weathered cheeks slightly flushed now. 'What the hell.'

'We might have sent Bastian after an innocent man, Amos.'

Amos looked over at him as if he had slapped him in the face. 'Innocent? A goddam bounty hunter? He still killed my boy, damn it.'

'But it would seem he's not a murderer, Amos. We should call Bastian off, I suppose. But we'd never get to him soon enough.'

Suddenly Amos rose to his feet. 'Call him off? Goddam it, Guthrie! What's gotten into you! You knew my boy! You don't care what happened to him?'

'Amos. It looks like Duke caused the trouble he got into. I don't think we owe him a payback, if Sloan is right.'

'That's it! How the hell do we know this Sloan is being truthful? Or even that he's who he says he is!' Now he fairly shouted at Guthrie. 'I'm not calling Bastian off! And neither are you!'

That outburst ended in a coughing fit that put Amos into his chair again. He looked bad. Guthrie bent over him and felt his pulse. Then he called for the house-keeper, and it was just a few minutes later when they got him upstairs and onto his wide bed.

Amos was looking very pale suddenly, and having trouble breathing. Guthrie loosened his clothing, and turned to the woman.

'You better send for the doctor. He's not looking so good.'

When she was gone, Guthrie sat on the edge of the bed. Amos was breathing harshly, and there was a rattling in his chest.

'Listen to me,' he croaked out.

'You better lay quiet, Amos.'

'You got to promise me.'

'Yes?'

'You got to promise. You won't try to get in touch with Bastian.'

Guthrie shook his head. 'Are you sure that's what you want?'

'Goddam it! Promise!' In a coughing yell.

Guthrie laid a hand on his shoulder. 'All right, Amos. I promise.'

Amos seemed to settle down then, but a moment later his eyes widened for a moment, and a great rattling came from his chest, and Amos Latham stopped breathing.

Guthrie sighed heavily, and placed his hand on Amos' chest. He shook his head slowly.

'It ain't your problem no more, Amos. Rest in peace.'

It was still that same evening in Birney Pass, and almost midnight. The Lakota Kid had had time to absorb the bad news that Certainty Sumner had followed him there, and was trying to decide what to do about it.

Sumner had arrived just an hour earlier, had gone directly to the small hotel down the street from the saloon, to check in and inquire about the Kid. Then he had decided to bed the stallion down before checking at the saloon. While there, he confirmed that the Kid's mount was already bedded there, and that gave him satisfaction. About that time the Kid was finding out that Sumner was in town. And it was an easy decision for him to do what he had intended at Smith's Crossing. He was going to take the fight to Sumner. In the same way, while the Kid was at the hotel checking on Sumner, Sumner learned that the Kid had just left the saloon.

And that was the situation that existed at midnight.

Sumner was becoming frustrated. He walked back down to the dark stables, and saw the Kid's mount still there. That puzzled Sumner. The men he hunted usually either fought or ran. And the Kid knew he was in town, they had told him so at the saloon. It seemed the Kid had decided to go into hiding.

The question was, where?

He was getting tired when he arrived back at the hotel. He just wanted this over with now. Especially with the possibility that he had Luther Bastian looking for him.

'Anybody been in here looking for me?' he asked the desk clerk when he arrived at the run-down, sleazy hotel.

'A couple of men was here. You just missed them.'

Sumner swore. 'Two men?'

'Yes, sir. I think one was that Lakota Kid.'

'Did they check in?'

'No, sir. They left. Would you like your key?'

Sumner sighed. The Kid could be anywhere. And it was a moonless night. 'Yes, give me my key.'

Then he was heading up to the second floor. It occurred to him that he could sleep at the hostelry, so he would know if the Kid was running. But he knew he was too tired for that. He could end up dead.

What Sumner didn't know was that the crafty Kid had

circled around to the back of the place with Dude, and they had come up a back stair and were now hiding in the shadows of an alcove across from Sumner's room.

Sumner was thinking of Dulcie as he approached his room, and was momentarily distracted from his surroundings. As he leaned forward to unlock the door, the Kid and Dude levelled their guns on him. But suddenly the Dardick was slippery-damp in the Kid's hand. Sumner's reputation was so formidable that even with this advantage, the Kid wasn't sure he would come out of this alive. Maybe disarming Sumner would be more certain than hoping that big Peacemaker didn't come into play. He laid his left hand on Dude's Colt to abort any action, and called out to Sumner just as Sumner was turning the key in the door.

'Don't move!'

Sumner froze in place, knowing exactly what was happening. He slumped slightly, blaming himself for his laxity. Tensing to turn and return fire when the Kid shot him. But that didn't happen.

'Don't even breathe. Move your hand away from that piece.'

Without hot lead hitting him, Sumner relaxed slightly. 'Pretty clever, Kid. Now what?' Moving his right hand away from the Colt.

'My friend is going to take that big gun. Don't try to stop him. This Dardick is aimed at your head.' He motioned Dude forward.

Dude ran his free hand over his mouth, which was dry. But he moved across the corridor warily. Sumner heard him coming, but the situation was dangerous. In a moment he felt Dude reach to slip the big gun from its holster, deciding to do nothing at that moment. Then the gun was gone. Dude stepped back, and slid the Peacemaker into his belt.

'Got it!' he said breathlessly to the Kid.

Sumner swore to himself. The weapon that made him so dangerous was gone. His only defence now was the one-shot Derringer in the custom holster at his back, under the dark jacket.

The Kid was grinning broadly now. He had out-smarted the great Sumner. Sumner was his, to do whatever he wished with him. He went over to Sumner, beside Dude. 'Well, Sumner. Looks like you came after the wrong boy this time.' Sumner had turned to face them. 'What do you think of the Lakota Kid now?'

Sumner smiled slightly. 'About the same as I did, I reckon. What are you up to, Kid? You want to steal my spurs first?'

'No, I've decided to enjoy this. Why don't we go on into your room? For a little privacy?'

Sumner had little choice with two guns on him. He turned, opened the door, and they all went into the small room. The Kid carefully closed the door behind them.

It was a grubby place, with an iron bed and a straight chair on a wall. 'You go over to the bed and remove that coat,' the Kid ordered him. 'Things can hide in coats.'

'Yeah, things can hide in them coats,' Dude echoed him.

Something released its hold on Sumner's insides. The Kid had just made a small mistake.

143

'When you get that off, we're going to play a little game,' the Kid grinned, completely relaxed now. 'I'm going to shoot you up a little at a time, and I'm going to let you tell me where to shoot first.'

'How nice for me,' Sumner said easily. He started removing the jacket. When it was gone, he would have access to the Derringer.

'Go get the jacket and throw it on that chair over there,' the Kid ordered Dude.

In the next few seconds things happened very fast. When Sumner reached behind him to remove the jacket, his hand came forward holding the Derringer. Dude was within arm's length, and his eyes widened as the pistol barked out loudly in his ears and put a blue hole in his forehead just between his eyes.

The Kid's eyes saucered too, and then he was firing the Dardick wildly at Sumner. But Dude hadn't fallen yet, and Sumner had taken one step forward and grabbed his Peacemaker from Dude's belt before he fell.

The Kid's shot grazed Sumner's neck, then the big Colt roared out in the small room twice, hitting the Kid in the left side and just under the heart.

The Kid just stood there for a moment, staring unbelieving at Sumner, then fell forwards on to his face, making the floor shake.

Sumner twirled the Colt backwards twice and let it nestle snugly into its oiled holster. He still looked as calm as if he had just prepared his bed for the night. He walked over to the very dead Kid.

'I should have told you, Kid. I don't play games.'

NINE

Early the next morning, Luther Bastian rode into town.

He was sure he would finally find Certainty Sumner here, and his mission would be finished, one way or the other.

He was right.

Sumner had got some sleep after all that night, after the hotel management had cleared his room of the bodies of the Kid and his cohort, and the incident had been reported to the part-time mayor.

Sumner felt inside him that the Preacher was closing in on him, but had no idea the confrontation between them would take place later that morning.

For Sumner, the whole thing was bewildering. He had no idea what it was all about. For the Preacher, it was a life climax. If he was successful, he could return to Maggie and Jonah and resume a life he had come to love. If he wasn't, he would have given his life for Jonah. And he would never see Maggie again.

It was a beautiful early summer morning. The sun had risen colourfully, striping the eastern sky with ribbons of pastel hues. The sleepy little town woke slowly, with no warning of what was about to happen to disturb its tranquillity.

A store owner came and unlocked his door for business. A farmer's wagon rumbled past laden with vegetables for sale in town. A yellow dog crossed the dusty street to find a sunny spot.

It was an ordinary day.

Until mid-morning.

Bastian had had a light breakfast at a small café, and then walked down the street to inquire at the just-opened saloon about Sumner. On the way, several town folk turned to stare at him because of his dangerous look, and one woman crossed the street to avoid him.

In the saloon, Bastian went up to the bar and ordered a beer. The bartender looked him over carefully. He didn't want any trouble from strangers looking like Bastian, especially after what he had gone through with the Kid on the previous night. He still didn't know the Kid was dead.

He delivered Bastian's beer and wiped off the bar with a towel. Bastian drank some of the beer, then spoke to him. 'There's a man named Sumner. He's supposed to be here in Birney Pass. Has he been in here?'

'Sumner? Why the hell would you want him? You a friend of his?'

Bastian gave him a stony look. 'I asked you a question. Have you seen him?' The bartender started to reply, when he looked past Bastian towards the door.

'Well, if that don't beat all. There he is right now.'

Sumner saw Bastian turn to him, and stopped where

he was. He sighed heavily. 'Sonofabitch,' he muttered.

Neither man went for his gun. 'So you're the Preacher,' Sumner said quietly.

'So you're Certainty Sumner.'

Sumner walked over to the bar and leaned on it not far from Bastian. 'I'll take what he's drinking,' he told the bartender.

Neither man spoke until Sumner had his beer. Bastian had drunk some more of his. Sumner took a drink too. The few patrons sitting nearby had heard the brief exchange, and all attention was now focused on the two gunslingers at the bar. The bartender suddenly understood the immeasurable significance of what was happening in front of him.

'Good God!' he muttered to himself, but very audibly in the new silence. 'Certainty Sumner and the Preacher!'

Bastian gave him a dark look.

'Holy Jesus!' From a nearby table.

'Why don't you go uncrate some whiskey?' Sumner said in that quiet voice.

The bartender licked dry lips and nodded. 'Yes, sir, Mr Sumner.'

Sumner took another sip of beer and turned to Bastian. 'You came all the way up from Texas for this?'

Bastian shrugged. 'It seemed worthwhile.'

Sumner nodded. 'I heard about that custom Colt on your belly there. How's the balance?'

'I like it. What do you think of the longer barrel?'

'It's never let me down.'

'That's what I hear. They say you can't be beat.'

147

Sumner grunted. 'Anybody can be beat. Do you like ranching?'

Bastian nodded. 'I've taken to it pretty well.'

'I heard you have a family down there.'

Bastian gave him a narrow look. 'That don't make any difference, Sumner.'

'I didn't think so. Or you wouldn't be here.'

'I own a nice little spread. Right on the river.'

Sumner sighed. 'I'm thinking of doing some ranching myself.'

Bastian looked over at him. 'That surprises me.'

'There's this girl. Her daddy is a rancher.'

'Ah.'

Sumner swigged some beer. 'Bastian, no offence, but I think you're a goddam fool.'

Bastian's long face didn't change. 'You're not the first.'

'Somebody put you on a wrong track. That dodger you have. It came from Arizona, didn't it?'

'That's right. And a good source.'

'You've been defrauded. I haven't been in Arizona for over two years.'

'I guess that's what I'd say. If I were you.'

Sumner was irritated. 'Where's the Wanted dodger?'

'Right here.' He took it from a pocket and handed it to Sumner. Sumner looked it over, and shook his head. 'This is pure bull-pucky. I don't know that lawman.' He dropped it on to the counter.

'I'm not here to argue a case,' Bastian said softly. 'That's for lawyers. I'm judge, jury and executioner. That's the way it is.'

148

'I've heard that about you. But you're making a big mistake.'

The bartender heard that, from down the bar. He called out to the other patrons. 'Oh, my God! Certainty Sumner against the Preacher! This is historic! This is a once-in-a-lifetime event!'

'Holy Christ!' a patron murmured.

Both Sumner and Bastian ignored them.

'You know I have to do this,' Bastian finally remarked.

Sumner nodded heavily. 'I know.'

'Listen, gentlemen,' the barkeep now said earnestly. 'Don't let it happen in here. Please! We just got shot up last night.'

Bastian finished his beer. Sumner hesitated a moment, and did the same.

'On the street,' Bastian said.

'I'll be there,' Sumner told him.

Bastian turned and walked past Sumner to the swinging doors, looking dark and ominous, and left the place. Before Sumner could follow, every patron in the saloon rose and hurried outside. And Sumner could hear them calling to other people on the street.

When Sumner got outside, there was a small crowd lining the dusty street. There was lots of animated talking, and a few bets were made. Bastian was waiting under a store canopy. Sumner saw him slide the custom Colt in and out of its holster a couple of times.

Sumner went down into the street to face him. Only thirty feet away. His long jacket pushed aside to reveal a dark red vest and the wicked-looking Peacemaker on his hip. Thirty feet away was Bastian, all in black, looking like an agent of the Devil himself. Nobody who had seen that stance had ever lived to describe it.

Bastian himself was tight inside. He had never faced an outlaw with this kind of reputation. He knew he was laying his life on the line for Jonah, and for his future.

Sumner was incapable of tension. Ever since that night with his aunt when he was just seventeen, and three men raped and murdered her in front of him, he had never been afraid again.

'Whenever you're ready,' he told Bastian in a level voice.

'I'm always ready,' was Bastian's response.

Sumner saw the slight change in the Preacher's eyes just before he made his move, which was fast as lightning.

In that split moment Sumner's hand suddenly had the Peacemaker in it and he had Bastian beat by a full second, the big gun flashing in the sun. Aimed at Bastian's heart.

He didn't fire.

Bastian saw he had been beaten. But he had never backed off a draw-down in his life. And he had made an unrescindable contract with Amos Latham. He had never welched on a contract.

He aimed at Sumner's chest to fire.

But Sumner had seen his eyes again, and the Peacemaker roared out in the silence of the street and punched Bastian like a baseball bat in the high chest, knocking him off his feet. He fell to the ground on his back, motionless.

Sumner came and stood over him as Bastian disarmed himself. 'By God you're good,' he grated out breathlessly, forcing a smile.

Sumner twirled the big gun over a couple of times and holstered it. 'Pretty much like you a while back,' he told him. He knelt over Bastian and examined the wound.

'It's in the high chest, near the shoulder. Right where I placed it. I don't think it hit bone. You'll be all right.'

'You could have killed me. Why didn't you?'

'It was Dulcie. She wouldn't have wanted me to.'

'The girl?'

Sumner nodded. He grabbed Bastian and helped him to his feet. Bastian stood dizzily. On the sides of the street, there were suddenly loud exclamations from the crowd. Then the bartender came rushing out, having missed the whole thing. He took a look at Bastian on Sumner's arm, and shook his head slowly. 'Hey, boys! I just showed this dodger you left on the bar to my manager! He knows that lawman in Arizona, and this ain't his signature!'

Sumner and Bastian stopped where they were, and Bastian turned to Sumner slowly. 'You're right. I have been a damn fool.'

'You had a lot of things pushing you,' Sumner offered.

'My God. I could have killed you.'

Sumner smiled. 'That's not likely, Preacher.'

Bastian returned the smile, and they proceeded on down the street to get Bastian's rare and historic wound tended.

*

By mid-afternoon Bastian had been seen by a local doctor who sought for, but did not find any lead in Bastian's chest. A big bandage was applied, and the patient was sent away with a bottle of laudanum for pain. In late afternoon Sumner visited him at the hotel before riding out. Bastian was in a room just down the hall from where Sumner had had to defend himself against the Kid the night before.

Bastian was propped up on his bed, and a room clerk had just left him a small bowl of soup, which he hadn't touched.

'Come past to see your handiwork?' he joked to Sumner.

'You're looking better already,' Sumner told him, standing beside his bed. 'Look. I just wanted to tell you there's no hard feelings. And when you get back to that wife and boy down there, say hey from Certainty Sumner.'

'I'll do that. And the same to that girl of yours.'

'I don't know yet she is mine,' Sumner said quietly. 'That's what I'll find out when I get there.' He tipped his Stetson. 'An honour to meet up with you, Preacher. I'll always remember it.'

'You gave me my life back,' Bastian said solemnly. 'I'll damn well never forget you.'

Sumner gave him a long look. Then, without speaking further, he turned and left the room.

He figured he would never see the Preacher again.

TEN

Despite the sunny summer day, Dulcie Provost was depressed. It was getting harder and harder to believe that Wesley Sumner was actually going to show up there one day.

It was almost a year now since he had received her farewell embrace and surprise kiss, and he had promised her that he would return one day to see how she still felt about him. As she had known at the time, despite her tender years, her feelings hadn't changed. In fact, she realized, she might be more in love with him now than she had been when she saw him ride off into his dangerous life.

It was late morning when Dulcie finished some chores inside the house and decided to walk to the stables to personally feed her favourite mount, a pinto pony stallion. When she arrived there, her one-time suitor Judd Owens was there talking with Jake Cahill, the ranch foreman. They both turned to watch Dulcie approach. Judd had given up on Dulcie when he realized her feelings for

Sumner, but just the sight of her now made him hunger inside for her.

'Hey! There's Dulcie! Looking more beautiful than ever!'

She forced a smile. 'Judd. What brings you over here?'

'He came to borrow some barbed wire,' Cahill answered for him. 'We just got it loaded aboard his wagon.'

'How's everything at the Bar J?' Dulcie asked to be polite.

'Oh, we're fattening them up pretty good, Dulcie.' He studied her lovely face. 'I'm glad to see you looking so great. I mean, you know, despite current circumstances.'

Dulcie gave him a narrow look.

'Well. I'm just saying. With all hope gone. You're holding up real well.'

'All hope gone?' Dulcie said darkly.

'Well, yes. About ever seeing that fellow Sumner again.'

Dulcie's face showed sudden anger. 'If you'll excuse me.' She went on into the stables, disappearing inside.

Judd looked over at Cahill. 'What did I say?'

Cahill was shaking his head. 'Never mind, Judd. But maybe you better avoid Dulcie for a while. When you stop past.' His face sombre.

'Well, sure,' Judd replied innocently. 'I was just sympathizing.'

A few minutes later he was gone on his wagon, and Dulcie emerged from the building. 'I'll walk you to the house,' Cahill told her.

As they walked, Cahill looked over at her. Judd had been right. Despite her depression over Sumner, she was still the loveliest girl in five counties. 'Dulcie, you have to get your mind on something else. With every day that passes the odds go up on Sumner's never arriving here. I know you don't want to hear that, but Maynard is beginning to worry over you.'

Dulcie's eyes went moist. 'It's just got hold of me, Jake. There doesn't seem to be much I can do about it.'

'You're not eating. You're not sleeping. You're giving us all a lot of concern. Think about it. What will you do if he never shows up?'

She looked over at him as they walked. 'I don't want to think about it.'

'At some point you may have to.'

'I can't let myself believe that. You've never seen him in action, Jake. I don't see how anybody could take Wesley Sumner down.'

'That's because of your feelings for him.'

'No. It's being impressed by what I saw. What I experienced. And besides, he promised me.'

Cahill smiled slightly. 'I understand, Dulcie.'

They had arrived at the house. 'I think I'll stay out here for a few minutes,' she told him, as they stood on the long porch with its Victorian balustrade.

Cahill nodded. 'I'll just go tell Maynard about Judd.'

After he left her, Dulcie went and leaned against the façade near the door. She sighed heavily. It took her down to talk about it. She had to defend a position that at times seemed indefensible.

After a few moments, Maynard Provost came out on to the porch and walked over to her.

'What's going on, daughter?'

Dulcie tried a smile. 'I'm just enjoying the summer day.'

'You don't look like you're enjoying it.' His silver hair shone in the morning sun.

'I'm doing my best, Papa.'

He saw that she was looking out past the big gate, a hundred yards away. 'You can't make him magically appear, you know. Just by staring out there.'

'I was thinking about the Wolf Creek crossing,' she said ruefully. 'And what started all this.'

Provost sighed. 'That was a day I'll never forget.'

'We got very lucky, Papa. When you ran into Wesley.'

'I'm very aware of that.'

Out by the bunkhouse, Corey Ross, the cowhand who had been with Dulcie on that fateful day, shouted to them.

'Rider coming!'

Dulcie's hope was so low that it didn't even occur to her to think of Sumner. 'I'll bet it's that damnable Judd Owens back,' she said darkly. 'You handle it, Papa.'

'No, wait. That's not Owens.' He squinted down. 'Oh, my God. Look at this!'

Dulcie focused on the rider, and at that moment, Ross yelled again. 'It's Sumner! It's by-God Sumner!'

Dulcie's breath sucked in without her knowing it. 'Oh, God! Oh, God, Papa!'

Provost watched the rider come into closer view, and

a heavy weight seemed to lift off his chest. Dulcie slowly slid to the floor of the porch, and began crying there. Out loud. Uncontrollably.

Provost knelt to comfort her, and put a hand on her shoulder. But she barely noticed. Sumner was in the yard now, and riding slowly up to the hitching rail. Jake Cahill was back out on the porch suddenly, and the bunkhouse was emptying out, with excited cowhands all looking towards Sumner.

Sumner had already seen Dulcie. Sitting there on the porch crying. Now she rose to her feet, her sobs waning. She wiped at her lovely face as it lit up like the morning sun. 'Wesley!' she cried out. 'It's really you!'

Sumner was tired from a long trip. But seeing Dulcie again, looking more beautiful than he remembered, the fatigue melted away.

He dismounted and touched the stallion's muzzle. 'Morning, Dulcie. Sorry I made you wait so long.' On the ground, with that artillery hanging from his belt, he looked just as dangerous as she remembered him.

He started towards the porch, but Dulcie was already halfway to him. When she arrived there she threw herself into his arms, and began kissing him over and over.

Sumner just stood there hugging her to him and enjoying it. He hadn't fully realized until that moment how much he wanted this. Or needed it.

'I guess that means you're still available,' he finally grinned at her.

'I would have waited forever,' she said, tears still running down her cheeks. 'Everybody said you were dead, but I never believed it.'

Sumner smiled at her. 'Didn't you know? There's nobody out there can kill me!'

He had meant it as a joke. But Dulcie nodded her head. 'I know that. That's what I told everybody that would listen.'

Provost and Cahill came down to them, and Cahill embraced Sumner for a moment. He tried to say something, but was too emotional. Provost came up and shook Sumner's hand. 'I always thought you'd be back. But you gave us some doubts there for a while.'

'I had some myself a couple of times,' Sumner admitted.

Several ranch hands had gathered out in the yard behind them. Staring in awe at Sumner as if he were a Washington celebrity.

'Did you really outgun Curly Quentin, Sumner?'

'They say you rode with Clay Allison.'

'Did you kill the Preacher?'

Dulcie stood there with a smug smile on her face. She exchanged a private look with her father.

Sumner turned to the onlookers. 'There'll be time for all of that later.' He turned back to Provost. 'It's damn nice to be back here, Provost.'

'I hope you intend to stay.'

'I just want two things now. Your daughter, and a job.'

Dulcie's smile widened even further. She took hold of his arm. 'I've waited a year to hear you say that!' Softly. Eyes moist again.

'It gives me much pleasure to offer you both,' Provost grinned at him. 'What about that?' He gestured towards

158

the big Colt on Sumner's hip.

'Oh, that,' Sumner said. He reached for the Peacemaker and drew it casually, and sent a small thrill of awe through Dulcie. 'I'm hoping I won't be needing this any more.'

As all present watched silently, Sumner slid the Colt back into its familiar resting place, and then unbuckled the wide leather gunbelt that held it. It came away with both the Colt and the Derringer from the back holster. There were a couple of low whisperings among the ranch hands.

Sumner wrapped the ammo belt and the guns into one tight bundle and handed it over to Provost. 'Here. Put this away somewhere for me. I hope I never need it again.'

Provost took the guns. He looked at them for a long moment, and nodded. They had saved his daughter's life less than a year ago. 'I'd guess you're making a good trade,' he grinned, glancing at Dulcie.

Sumner put an arm over her shoulder. 'The best one of my life,' he replied. For the first time since his aunt's murder, he felt he was exactly where he wanted to be. Where he was supposed to be.

Dulce felt a tightness in her throat. Sometimes miracles seemed to come from nowhere. 'You're home, my love. You're really home.'

'And it will be yours as long as you want it,' Provost added.

At that moment the new, beautiful truth crashed in on Sumner like a summer storm, even though it had brewed in him all the way there. He didn't have to be

Certainty Sumner any more. That world was gone forever and would never exist for him again.

He had fulfilled a well hidden but life-saving dream.